J
WIS

Wisler, G. Clifton

7/88

This new land

110567

$14.85

DATE			

DISCARDED

X

Walker's American History
series for young people

This
New Land

Walker's American History
Series for Young People

NONFICTION

Incredible Constructions and the People Who Built Them
Mel Boring
Mississippi Steamboatman: The Story of Henry Miller Shreve
Edith McCall
Mysteries in American Archeology
Elsa Marston
Who Put the Cannon in the Courthouse Square?
A Guide to Uncovering the Past
Kay Cooper

FICTION

Away to Fundy Bay (Nova Scotia, 1775)
Katherine McGlade Marko
Message from the Mountains (Missouri, 1826)
Edith McCall
Straight Along a Crooked Road (crossing America, 1850)
Marilyn Cram Donahue
The Valley In Between (California, 1857–1860)
Marilyn Cram Donahue
The Stratford Devil (Connecticut, 1651)
Claude Clayton Smith
What About Annie? (Maryland, the Great Depression)
Claudia Mills
Which Way Freedom? (South Carolina, 1861–1864)
Joyce Hansen

This
New Land

G. Clifton Wisler

Walker and Company
New York

Walker's American History Series for Young People
Frances Nankin, Series Editor

First published in the United States of America in 1987 by the Walker Publishing Company, Inc.

Published simultaneously in Canada by Thomas Allen & Son Canada, Limited, Markham, Ontario.

Library of Congress Cataloging-in-Publication Data

Wisler, G. Clifton.
    This new land / G. Clifton Wisler.
        p. cm.—(Walker's American history series for young people)
    Bibliography: p.
    Summary: Ten-year-old Richard Woodley describes his trip to the New World aboard the Mayflower and tells about the first year spent by the Pilgrims at Plymouth.
    ISBN 0-8027-6726-5. ISBN 0-8027-6727-3 (lib. bdg.)
    1. Pilgrims (New Plymouth Colony)—Juvenile fiction. 2. Mayflower (Ship)—Juvenile fiction. 3. Plymouth (Mass.)—History—Juvenile fiction. [1. Pilgrims (New Plymouth Colony)—Fiction. 2. Mayflower (Ship)—Fiction. 3. Plymouth (Mass.)—History—Fiction.] I. Title. II. Series.
    PZ7.W78033Tg 1987
    [Fic]—dc19   87-17749
                                                                        CIP
                                                                        AC

Book design by Laurie McBarnette
Cover Illustration by Beth Peck.

Printed in the United States of America

for Jacque, Kay, and the gang at
Bowman Middle School

TABLE OF CONTENTS

AUTHOR'S NOTE

Today we call them pilgrims, those hundred men, women, and children who set sail on the *Mayflower* in hopes of finding a new and better life in the Americas. They faced a perilous voyage across the Atlantic in a small wooden ship. The captain relied on the stars and a primitive compass for guidance and on the whims of the wind for power. Half died the first winter.

Why did they come? What inner strength enabled them to carve a new world from the hostile wilderness?

First, it is important to understand that the *Mayflower's* company consisted of two different groups, the Strangers and the Saints. The Saints made up the largest and best-known party. They were commonly called Separatists, because they wished to break away from the Church of England. King James I of England and Scotland, whose Catholic mother, Mary Queen of Scots, was executed by his Protestant cousin, Queen Elizabeth, began his rule in a spirit of religious toleration. James I sought to unify his two kingdoms with their two faiths, and he even had the Bible translated from the Latin used by Catholics to the English used by Protestants, creating the famous King James version. Later, however, James's ministers convinced him that Separatists posed a threat to his royal authority since they held their beliefs above the king's laws. Separatists were forced to worship in secret, and those discovered were often imprisoned. Many fled the kingdom.

These Separatists, or Saints, believed the Bible was the sole guide and authority for their lives. They refused to practice many of the sacraments ordained by the Church of England. They also refused to be governed by ministers or bishops, and they respected none appointed by the king. They met in common houses or out in the open. They kept the Sabbath, meaning they devoted Sunday entirely to prayer and Scripture reading. No work was performed, and no play was tolerated.

Being a boy, like Richard Woodley, must have been very hard. The Saints expected their children to obey the Ten Commandments, and punishment for telling a lie or disobeying parents was often very severe. Boys had to study Scripture nightly. All children had to work long and hard. Singing, other than hymns, and games involving chance were considered the devil's temptations, and punishment was sure to follow.

The Strangers, on the other hand, were common Englishmen who were taken aboard the *Mayflower* when it became clear more money was needed to fund the voyage than could be provided by the Saints alone. In addition, some Strangers, like Captain Myles Standish, had special talents or crafts that would be needed in the new settlement. Most yearned for a fresh start. They came from all manner of backgrounds and worshipped different faiths.

It must have been difficult for boys like Richard to witness other children, first in the Netherlands and later aboard the *Mayflower*, who did not face the same strict rules of behavior. For instance, though his father surely explained why the Saints didn't celebrate Christmas, Richard might have envied the Strangers who enjoyed the holiday from work.

In writing *This New Land*, I have attempted to tell a story of courage, of how, faced with even the greatest hardships, people demonstrating faith and self-sacrifice managed to prevail. From my first visit to Plymouth, Massachusetts, on a gale-swept June morning in 1977, I was captured by the story of what had happened there in 1620. I returned in 1983 and again in 1984 to learn more, and it was during my days of speaking to the historians at Plimoth Plantation that Richard Woodley began to take life. I watched boys and girls weave thatch, and I saw craftsmen rive and join planks as Richard's father might have done 367 years ago.

It was not until I began exploring William Bradford's diary, though, written in an unfamiliar prose style and etched with pain and loss, that I began to understand the price paid by those early settlers of Plymouth.

There is a simple plaque on a quay in Plymouth, England, which tells how the *Mayflower* set sail from that place bound for America. Last March I stood there watching a modern fishing boat slip past the jetty on its way to the outer harbor. People strolled by, but few realized the significance of that place in another

time. It's my hope that this story will serve as a reminder.

G. Clifton Wisler
Garland, Texas
April 17, 1987

This
New Land

ONE
THE ADVENTURE BEGUN

I remember very clearly the first time my father spoke of leaving Leyden. It was a dreary spring day, shrouded in a heavy mist that had blown in off the North Sea. I was about my usual afternoon duties, pushing a cart of wool down the narrow, muddy streets. Houses rose above me, one atop another, so that I had the feeling someone was forever watching my every move, and I was ever alert lest a crock of potato peelings or stale water should rain down upon me.

I prayed that the mongrel dogs which haunted the area would not mistake me for the butcher's boy. A fortnight earlier a large terrier had torn my best leather stockings and left my shins bleeding from a dozen bites.

At such times I found it difficult to keep faith with the Commandments. Many boys in Leyden, as elsewhere in the free Netherlands, busied themselves playing games or employing themselves in the devil's business, stealing pies from the bakery or partaking of strong drink at the alehouse. Those whose fathers belonged to the trade guilds often visited the library of the great university. I had heard from Elder Brewster that there were walls of books there, though I doubted it. I had never seen more than a score in one place and could not imagine such. As for journeying to the library myself, Father would have decried the wastefulness of such a trip, and I had to content myself with borrowing a volume as chance permitted. Of course, I had my dreams, but they had no need of pages or writing.

When I spoke of the hardships of our life in Leyden, my father would quote from Proverbs 22: "Folly is bound up in the heart of a child, but the rod of discipline drives it from him."

Father was fond of his Bible. Often he read to us from Job or Lamentations. But he favored Proverbs.

"He who keeps his mouth and his tongue keeps himself out of trouble," he said to me more than once, pointing to the twenty-first verse. "Richard, never you mind the idle talk of the wicked and the sloth."

Still it was hard to witness the laughter of the town boys when they watched us toiling all the day at such lowly tasks as weaving coarse cloth or shoveling dung from the stableyards.

"Once we lived a most different life," my elder sister, Mary, told me the day I returned torn and bleeding with the wool. Five years my senior, Mary delighted in telling me what I did not know. "I remember Grandfather's great house in Yorkshire," she continued, "surrounded as it was with fields of golden wheat and great oak forests. For dinner we would enjoy great stews filled with carrots and peas."

My eyes widened.

"It will not always be as it is," Mother told us when

the winter winds whined through the attic room I shared with my brothers. "The Lord promises bounty to he who is content to wait."

"Wait how long?" I asked. I had no memories of England, having been born in Amsterdam the first winter of our migration to the Netherlands. My father sold all he had to escape the king's soldiers. We came to live in poverty, strangers in a foreign land. Returning to England would have meant imprisonment or perhaps worse.

"It is because of our faith that we are persecuted," Father told me when I had not yet reached my seventh birthday.

As I grew older, I was allowed to study with the elders. I never learned to read Greek and Latin as my friend Thomas Cushman or the Brewster boys did, but I was considered quick enough to read Scripture and write an educated hand. In time I discovered why Father and Mother had left England.

"The gospel is set forth in testament," Elder Brewster told me. "Bishops and priests are Roman inventions. We have none. We do not observe a sacrament which is not found in Scripture. King James, being the head of the Church of England, refuses to allow those who believe as we do to separate ourselves. He would rule our faith as he rules the land. We are called separatists and deemed traitors. Many have been sent away to prisons."

Elder Brewster had once been a man of great wealth. He had studied at the great university of Cambridge. But when he first attempted to leave England, he was arrested. Only after a second failure did the elder successfully reach the Netherlands.

Father was able to buy passage aboard a Dutch ship for himself, Mother, and Mary. In the dead of night they stole aboard. They were fortunate. Some ships' masters turned over their passengers to the king's soldiers. In such a case, Father would have forfeited all possessions and likely been thrown into a dungeon for months.

"So," Elder Brewster once told me, "as with the saints of old, we were hunted and imprisoned for our faith's sake. That is why some of us now call ourselves Saints."

Father had said as much himself. Mary once showed me a picture of a saint shot with arrows and another burned alive. It was not a happy thought, and I was glad Father had sailed.

The Netherlands seemed an ideal haven. The leading merchants, who called themselves burghers, welcomed us to Amsterdam and later to Leyden. Catholic Spain had ruled the low countries with an unyielding hand until recent times, and the Dutch had learned to be tolerant. But though we could worship in our own manner, we were allowed only menial employment. Guild membership was denied. Father, once a landowner in Yorkshire, was forced to become a weaver of wool. Boys had to toil long hours at hard labor.

"It is good for a man that he bear the yoke in his youth," Father read from Lamentations.

I was aged but twelve years, though. Each night I lay on a straw bed with my brothers, Thomas and Edward, huddling together against the bitter cold. It was difficult to feel blessed when freezing. Did not Job doubt himself at times?

The thought of those frigid nights never quite left my mind. I shivered as I pushed the heavy wool cart, keeping alert lest the dogs catch me unawares. As it turned out, I arrived home unmolested. My brother Edward stood at the foot of the narrow stair that led to our small rooms atop what had once been a carpentry shop. Together we hauled the bundles of wool to the box Father had placed between the fireplace and his weaving loom.

Edward had always been a frail child, and though he was only two years younger than I, Father forbade him accompanying me on my labors. Our wee sister Susanna had taken a fever three winters past and died of it. So it was that Edward and little Thom, who was five, occupied themselves readying the wool for the loom or doing other work Father found suitable to their abilities.

"There is much to be said for finding a more permanent home for the congregation," Father was saying to our friend and neighbor John Goodman when I arrived. "It is not fitting that our people be subjected to such mean livelihoods as we can find here."

"Yes," Weaver Goodman agreed. "Look to our children. My boys have never seen an English countryside. The young ones speak German and French better than our own tongue."

"And these Dutchmen have no morals!" Father complained. "The young are about on the Sabbath, and their public behavior is an abomination. Young boys and girls keeping company in public houses!"

"There is much talk of Guiana," Weaver Goodman said. "The English gentleman Sir Walter Raleigh speaks highly of its wealth and temperate climate."

"Yet there are stories of great hardship there," Father said. "Even cannibalism."

"Virginia, then. There is a call from the Virginia Company for colonists."

"Aye, but we would be obligated to sign papers binding us to the Church of England. I have heard talk that Separatists in the Americas have been punished most cruelly by the Crown."

In the days which followed, few hours passed without some such conversation. Among my friends, feeling ran strong for emigration. It was already spring, however, and we knew that no successful colony had set out for the far shore of the Atlantic after the planting season had passed.

"My father says we are to go first to England, then on to America," Thomas Cushman told me as we waited together outside Elder Brewster's house. It was our day to read English history.

"Then it's to be Virginia," I sighed. "Father says the people there have hearts hardened against Saints."

"Trust the elders to find us a place with rich fields and fair neighbors," Thomas said. He had a confidence I always supposed came with being thirteen. More likely it grew of his being an only son in a motherless household.

"So long as there are no guilds," I said. "Or dogs."

"But John Goodman has dogs," Thomas objected.

"I will tolerate them," I said. "So long as they keep their teeth to themselves."

I spoke to Father about Virginia when I returned from Elder Brewster's house.

" 'Tis likely little more than talk," Father told me. "I have been told we would take ship to Guiana, to Virginia, even to Spanish Florida. It would be most unlikely that we would receive a kind welcome at the hands of the Inquisition!"

Indeed. For as I discovered on that Sabbath, the strongest arguments put forth for our departure concerned the Spanish. A great war had been fought for possession of the Netherlands only just before my birth. A twelve-year truce had been signed, but now it was due to expire. Some of the older boys among the congregation had already taken to the profession of arms.

"A prudent man sees danger and hides from it," the elders said, quoting from Father's favorite, Proverbs 22. So it was that those among us who still possessed property undertook the task of arranging backers and obtaining a charter from the Virginia Company.

I, of course, knew little of this. Only my friendship with Thomas Cushman provided a hint of what was to come. Father had reconciled himself to another winter in Leyden, and Edward and I did our best to employ ourselves to good effect with the coming of summer in hope of having a bit of wood for the fireplace come October.

Then, as suddenly as a stroke of lightning from the heavens, Father announced we would travel to Delft Haven. There we would board a ship for England.

"Will we visit Grandfather?" Mary asked. "Can we stay for a time on his farm?"

"It will be a long and arduous journey," Father warned us. "We must walk twenty-five miles just to the harbor, a distance as great as that to Amsterdam. From there we sail to Southampton."

"But can we not see Grandfather?" Mary asked.

"There will be time only for provisioning the ship," Father explained. "Yorkshire is many leagues to the north. As for your grandfather, our arrival would no doubt bring the attention of the king's soldiers. That would be a poor reward to offer a man who never closed his door or his purse to us in time of need."

We occupied ourselves many days preparing for the trek from Leyden to the sea. What few possessions could not be carried in the wool cart had to be sold at whatever meager sum could be got. Mother collected every scrap of clothing we owned and arranged bundles for each one of us to carry. Father obtained an extra pair of shoes for all from a cobbler. Shoes, he said, were most difficult to come by in the Americas.

Mother insisted on taking her great iron kettle, but most of her wooden platters were bartered for tools. Father obtained a fine iron breastplate, a cutlass, and a musket, partly through the efforts of Master Cushman, who was well acquainted with soldiers. I myself traded a bit of woodcutting for a fine blade of Toledo steel no doubt stolen from a Spanish dragoon. A man about to embark on a dangerous enterprise did well to go armed.

Alas, even with my dagger I remained but a boy of twelve. As such, I was subjected to every manner of human torment in those final days in Leyden. Mother thrice pricked me with a needle while fashioning a new shirt of brown wool for me, and Mary took her shears and clipped my hair. Edward and I looked with dismay at the great pile of flaxen hair about the floor and sighed. Little Thom was nigh certain Mary had cut an ear off his head. He was most relieved to find both were still attached.

"Far greater hardships lie in store for us, I fear," Mother said when I complained. "You should thank your sister for taking such care. She has a gentle touch with children, does Mary."

For myself, I would have chosen a different word perhaps. But Mother clearly had no patience for my complaints, and so I kept them to myself.

The morning of our departure, I assembled my brothers, and we began carrying our bundled possessions down to the wool cart. Mother shook her head and grumbled that we looked more scarecrow than children, for Mary's clipping had caused Edward's hair to jut out from beneath his hat like old straw. I feared I was no better, and my ill-fitting coatsleeves were rolled twice so my hands could function.

"The Lord cares little for vanity," Father said as he straightened Edward's collar. "That coat will keep out the chills of the sea breezes, Richard."

I dropped my chin and nodded. As we started down

the narrow street, I tried to close my ears to the taunts of the town boys. I knew nothing of the Americas, and yet I felt glad of the chance to leave Leyden behind.

Soon we joined the others on the dusty road to Delft Haven. I aided Father in pulling the cart while Mother and Mary alternately carried or led little Thom. Edward walked at my side, burdened with two bundles of cloth thought by Father appropriate to his size and ability.

It was an uneventful journey, if somewhat tiresome.

"I will rejoice at leaving this flat, barren land," Mary remarked once when she took my turn with the cart. "Yorkshire was ever so green and full of hills and valleys. I have heard it said Virginia is such a land."

"Thomas Cushman says Virginia is a country full of savages," I said as I heaved little Thom atop my shoulders.

"They are the Lord's people, Richard," Mary scolded. "We will find our way there, even as we did in Leyden."

"I pray we'll have better fortune."

"I, too," she said, grinning, as Thom made a face.

"You spoil that boy," Mother said as she urged us onward. "And you do your shoulders no great kindness, Richard."

In truth I did ache some, and I remembered Father quoting Lamentations. But we were only beginning our time of hardship. I could see no great harm growing from giving Thom a little comfort.

The ship was waiting when we arrived at Delft Haven. It was a fine-looking vessel of some sixty tons, called

Speedwell by her owners. Most of our cargo and provisions would be loaded in Southampton, as our benefactors and many of the ship's passengers waited there. Even so, our part of the congregation of Saints had its share of personal property to get aboard. Each trunk or bundle had to be ferried to the *Speedwell* in small boats. The loading required great effort and much patience. When all at last was put in its place, we gathered ashore for prayer and meditation.

Many of our friends came to bid us a safe voyage. Some made the long march from Leyden. Others came from Amsterdam. There was some weeping, especially among the children whose parents were going on ahead of them. I was glad to be setting out with Mother and Father, Mary and my brothers. Together we had overcome the greatest adversities, and I knew we would conquer those which lay ahead.

I do not remember all that was said by the elders in the time before our departure, but I do remember that much of the Book of Ezra was read. When the final farewells were said, *Speedwell* set sail, clearing the coast of the Netherlands on 22 July, the year of our Lord 1620.

It was a pleasant and speedy voyage into the North Sea and across the English Channel to the port of Southampton. Thomas Cushman and I spent our time climbing the rigging or keeping watch in the crow's nest for pirates. There was little danger in those waters now, but the mates kept us entertained with terrible tales of death on the high seas, and our imaginations took us off with great buccaneers on countless adventures. One time we sailed with Sir Francis Drake against the Spanish Armada. Another time we explored the barren north with Sir Martin Frobisher.

One calamity did befall me. Although he was mostly a serious boy, prone more to Latin and Greek than pranks, Thomas Cushman conspired with the helmsman to get me soaked through to the skin trying to reach the spritsail* in a heavy swell.

"It's an old enough trick," the sailors told me afterward. "It does work well on a landlubber, though."

The weather was fair, and we kept to the open deck whenever possible. *Speedwell* had never been designed for so many passengers, and belowdecks was cluttered with clothing, makeshift beds, and dozens of people. There was no chance for privacy.

"Father says we will be joined by a second ship at Southampton," Thomas told me as we sat together high above the deck beside the mainsail yard.

I was glad. The notion of sailing to Virginia in such close quarters was not an easy one to stomach. Thomas sensed my thoughts.

It was at Southampton that our trials began. It took a great deal of time to provision *Speedwell* and her consort, a large vessel of 180 tons christened *Mayflower*. There were problems with the accounts, and we began to worry.

In order to relocate ourselves in Virginia, Elder

---

*The sprit—a stout wooden pole—extends over the bow of such ships as *Speedwell*, and supports the spritsail, or bowsprit.

Brewster and others, including Thomas's father, had contracted with a Master Weston and a group of London merchants. We pledged to share our profits from seven years' labor with these gentlemen, who in turn funded our journey. But when costs for provisions ran high, these merchant adventurers, as they were called, refused to provide added capital. There were other disagreements as well.

It had been hoped that our colony would consist of Saints and no others, but we discovered a large group of passengers waiting in Southampton. Some forty were "Strangers," simple farmers and craftsmen who responded to the opportunity to sail to the New World and a new life. A few belonged to the Church of England. Worse, there were others who had no religious faith to speak of.

"I am sure some of them would as soon cut your throat as sing a hymn," Thomas told me. "I have heard less profanity from behind the doors of the alehouses in Leyden."

I spent little time concerning myself over the Strangers, however. They were assigned to *Mayflower*. *Speedwell* carried mostly Saints like ourselves, save for some of the servants and relations brought along by the wealthier families.

It seemed an eternity before the last of the provisions were made fast, and our two gallant ships moved out to sea. Once clear of land, we hoped for a swift journey. Soon, however, disturbing news spread throughout our ship. The master and his crew cursed and complained. *Speedwell*, for all her seeming grace and stoutness, was a ship plagued by leaks. Water continued to seep through her planking in spite of repeated efforts at bracing and caulking. Finally, in desperation, Mr. Reynolds, the master, put into Dartmouth harbor.

While Master Jones aboard *Mayflower* looked on from the deck of his more seaworthy ship, the crew of *Speedwell* plugged leaks and pumped bilgewater. When it appeared at last that both ships were able to bear up to the wilds of the Atlantic, we set sail again.

We were no more than a hundred leagues outbound when the leaking resumed. Nary a soul aboard the ship was dry. *Speedwell* was down by the bow, and more than a few of us prayed we would not sink. To make matters worse, the ship was unstable. It rocked constantly back and forth, and those not used to such antics were set upon by that scourge of sea voyages, seasickness.

Thomas and I suffered little of it. The sailors said it was due to our frequent climbing of the rigging, and some others tried it as a cure. It proved very little success, and most grew only worse for having tried. Many among the passengers pleaded for a gentler passage, but Master Reynolds had graver concerns. He finally was forced to put about and make for Plymouth. *Mayflower* followed closely.

Some claimed that the master and crew of *Speedwell* were far from disappointed to return. When their ship was inspected at Plymouth, no new leaks were discovered. Instead the ship was declared generally unseaworthy, either from poor construction or the strain of excess sail. The elders met and decided there was little prospect of *Speedwell* completing her crossing. Further delays would prove fatal to the colony's chances of survival. August was dying, and it would soon be fall. A winter landing promised disaster, and already we were eating into our stores.

It was decided that *Speedwell* should return to London. *Mayflower* would take on those passengers and supplies who chose to continue their journey to Virginia.

I left *Speedwell* reluctantly. I had grown accustomed to her, knew her crew, could navigate her decks in the dark. *Mayflower* was a much larger vessel. She now carried 102 passengers, most of them crammed together " 'tween decks," as the sailors called the space beneath the main deck. Saints and Strangers alike spread straw beds or arranged planks into bunks. A few of the wealthier families shared a cabin astern. The crew squeezed into the forecastle while the ship's officers berthed in the steerage cabin.

The heaviest blow to befall me came when I discovered my good friend, Thomas Cushman, was among those returning to London.

"I must accompany my father," Thomas told me as we said our farewell aboard *Mayflower*. "God grant you a fair wind. If fortune smiles on us, we will follow later."

But as I stood beside the foremast when the ship set sail from Plymouth, I wondered if we would find that fair wind. And if not, what disappointment lay in store for us next?

TWO
ASEA

Mayflower proved to be a wonder. She carried three times the cargo *Speedwell* bore, and her great sails drove us through the Atlantic swells as a hawk soars on a summer breeze. Her broad beam and deep draft kept her decks even, with only a gentle swaying. It was a pleasant change from the rocking, rolling motion of the *Speedwell*.

The ship's master, Christopher Jones, was a compassionate man who did what was within his power to ease our difficulties. He was a quarter owner of *Mayflower* and seemed to know the great ship's every plank and yard. Father explained that instead of taking us south to the Canary Islands on the normal route across the Atlantic, Master Jones would keep us north. We would miss the normal trade winds, but we would likewise avoid French and Spanish privateers. It might prove to be a more difficult voyage, but the savings in time at this late season promised to be worth the travail.

Each day Master Jones checked our course with his cross-staff. He then applied figures in an almanac and marked our progress on a sea chart. Even the elders were surprised at his grasp of mathematics and his strange ability to note the distance the ship made each day. Our confidence in the ship and its master grew greater each day we were at sea.

The mates, Master Clarke and Master Coppin, had both been to the Americas before. Their stories of great fishes and painted savages were both exciting and terrifying. Master Clarke could be relied upon for a fine tale of the sea when not occupied with the management of the ship, and more than once he showed Edward and me the workings of yards and lines. Soon I was able to distinguish clewline from buntline, leachline from lack. The mates had us tying sheet bend and bowline with ease before we had passed a week at sea.

Some of the sailors were less friendly, however. The bosun delighted in taunting us when we were about our prayers. He also tormented the sick, calling them all manner of names, and often threatened some small boy who was too slow in moving from a passageway.

My brother Edward and others among the passengers were in constant fear of that bosun. On one occasion Edward and I were climbing the rigging to have a look at the far horizon. Master Coppin gave us leave to do so, and some of the sailors joined us. The bosun had scant use for our adventure, though, and when Edward jumped to the deck, he was greeted with agitated curses.

"Move ye landlubbin' feet, boy!" the bosun cried, applying the tip of his boot to Edward's hip. "This is my deck! Step smartly here else I feed ye to the fishes!"

"He's done nothing!" I shouted from the rigging. "Leave him be!"

"Why, you whelp!" the bosun answered. "Come

down here and I'll boot the both of you below decks where you belong!"

I stayed in the rigging until the villain retired. Later Father spoke to Master Jones of the event. Master Coppin told me the master spoke most forcefully to the crew, but even so many of the sailors continued to torment us. The twenty ordinary seamen of the crew were especially prone to wild talk, and Father often lectured Edward and me on the evils of lewd behavior.

"These men have never had the good fortune to practice godly ways," Father said. "We must pray for their souls."

"Yes, Father," I answered respectfully. But neither Edward nor I would voice a prayer on behalf of the bosun. We did pray for deliverance from his evil ways.

The sailors were also not accustomed to the presence of women on ocean voyages, and unmarried girls such as Mary were seldom allowed above deck unescorted by their fathers or one of the elders.

"I do believe all the vilest men in England must have signed aboard this ship," Mary remarked to me one evening when we unfolded bedding for our family. "Nary a one has a civil tongue, and few possess the least sense of modesty."

"Yes," I agreed. "Master Jones says they are an unrefined lot, but they work hard, and we will soon be rid of them."

"Not soon enough," Mary grumbled.

I sat beside her for a time in hope of comforting her. 'Tween decks was a dark and damp place, and I knew it plagued her to be kept so long from the sunshine.

In Leyden she was forever planting flowers to lift our spirits and vanquish our despair. She twisted strands of her long yellow hair around her fingers and hummed a hymn. Then, for a time, she spoke of her memories of Yorkshire.

"Virginia will be like that," she whispered as she stroked my hair. "You and Father will have horses to ride, and we will have a house all to ourselves."

"And you will have a hundred suitors come to call," I said, grinning as her face grew pink. She pretended anger, but I could tell my words cheered her.

While Mary and the other girls were watched most closely, we boys, when not burdened by our lessons or another duty, were given leave to roam the ship. What hours of freedom were allowed came as a great relief to me. Our small corner 'tween decks was most miserable, even in fair weather. Father and Mother occupied the ground bunk. Mary had the good fortune to share a nearby berth with Elizabeth Tilley, a friend from Leyden and better company than brothers. Edward, Thom, and I spread ourselves out on the deck as best as we could, often huddling together under all our bedding. Even so, we were rarely warm. When the sea was heavy or a storm raged, we would be peppered with water seeping through the planking or blown down through an open hatch. It was not possible to remain dry, and there was no respite from the soaking till the Lord saw fit to send us sunshine.

In this confinement lay more than ninety of our company. At night the sounds of heavy breathing, coughing, and retching were more than one could stand. Children would whine, and sailors would shout down curses from their forecastle cabin. Two tin pails were provided for our bodily wastes and for the use of the sick. These were hardly sufficient for our numbers, and when the deck pitched in a storm, the buckets would spill their contents on some nearby innocent.

The elders and a few others lived better. They shared the great cabin, high up in the stern. I confess I was most sinfully envious of the Brewsters, especially Love and Wrestling, Elder Brewster's two boys. Both were younger than Edward. Their clothes were fine and new, and they never awoke wet and frozen.

As for myself, I rarely awoke otherwise. Whenever the ship rose and fell violently, Edward came crashing into me. Little Thom was often trapped between us, and he would whine like one of the pigs in the cargo. In the dead of night, showered by seawater and shivering from the cold, the entire company would moan and cry as one. I found myself remembering verses from Job and praying the Lord might forgive my weakness.

Even in the midst of our growing despair and hardship, we suffered no deaths. We reasoned this was due to our constant attention to prayer. Master Jones attributed it to *Mayflower's* history, however. The ship had been engaged twelve years in the Mediterranean wine trade, and leaking casks had given the timbers a sweet smell. I often noticed also the odors of tar, turpentine, and fish, combined with damp hemp, but there were few traces of the vile stenches rumored to carry plagues through the merchant fleets.

We occasionally caught sight of a rat, but the ship's cats were constantly on the prowl for such creatures.

Having encountered rats in our attic in Leyden, I was relieved we were spared a like ordeal at sea.

Some of our companions never overcame their seasickness, but most grew used to the motion of our ship. A third of all *Mayflower* passengers were children, and many of these were Strangers. I occupied many afternoons acquainting myself with my fellows, engaging them in races through the ship's rigging or contests of strength or daring.

Among the most mischievous aboard were the Billington boys, Francis and John. One day while partaking of a merry game of squibs below decks, they set a small fire near one of the powder casks. Only the quickest action by others of our company saved *Mayflower* from having her timbers scattered to the four winds, not to mention the fate that might have awaited us.

Francis was but eight years old, and John was scarcely six. Still, crew and company alike delighted in their howls as a rod was applied liberally to their backsides.

Also among the Strangers was one Myles Standish, appointed captain of militia. He was fond of relating his adventures as a lieutenant in Queen Elizabeth's army in the Netherlands' campaigns against King Philip of Spain. Captain Standish was nigh as tall as Mary, a little over five feet, but his flowing red hair and scarlet beard lent force to his words.

"I also have attended university," the captain told Elder Brewster when the two discussed the need of military drill aboard ship. "The university of war."

Captain Standish was brought along to train the men in musketry and sword play. Many times I sat with the other boys and watched as the captain demonstrated the way he had run Spaniards through with his sword in the late fighting. He also was a fine marksman, even on the deck of a pitching ship. After listening to the mates' tales of pirates, I rested better knowing boarders would have to face the rage of the little captain.

When Father had little for me to do, I would set off in search of adventure. On one such journey I came upon the cooper, John Alden. He was busy mending barrels, but even so, he found time to introduce me to his craft. I soon discovered that though John was twenty-one, he was more boy than man in his mind. I visited him often thereafter. He delighted in heaving me atop stacks of casks and barrels with his great strong arms. I would then inspect the bindings to ensure there were no leaks.

Occasionally John and I would locate a bad barrel. Then we would have to repair the damage or relocate the cargo. It was not always easy work, but John's speech remained soft and patient, even when I was less than perfect in my efforts.

Mary was clearly taken with him as well. She would question me about him when I returned from my coopering, then speak of his great blond hair and wonder if he spoke of her.

"Alas, he speaks only of barrels," I told Mary. Her disappointment was extreme.

Eating aboard ship was another grave trial. There was scant variety, and often little quantity or quality. Our mainstay was "salt horse," chunks of pickled beef or pork served with sea biscuit or "hardtack," as the sailors called it. We often ate dried fish and cheese as well. Those in the great cabin enjoyed some fruit and often sweetened their meal with sugar. We had no such luxuries.

Mother and the other women would often use the small oven to cook a bit of flour or stew some of the beef. But it was difficult to keep a fire lit with so much water dripping, and the danger of setting the ship's timbers alight prevented a fire being built elsewhere.

"Ay, what I'd offer for a fine leg of roast mutton," Captain Standish remarked to us one bright day. "My Rose is a fine one with peas and a carrot or two. I'll wager King James would not turn away from such a feast."

Wagering was forbidden us, and when Father heard me repeat the captain's words to Edward, I was visited by the rod. Still, my belly often wondered if it would ever again be treated to anything not cold and salted.

We sailed upon fine autumn breezes toward the latter part of our voyage. Master Jones had marked us past mid-ocean, and now it was only a matter of holding on till we reached the Virginia shore. Later the winds grew less steady, and we were forever tacking first in one direction, then in another. At such times all able-bodied men and boys would lend their arms to the braces.

First would come the call from Master Jones:

"All hands on deck!"

The mates would haul in the forty-foot lateen sail so that it stood tight against the mizzen mast. This maneuver would bring the stern of the ship around. Next the large square spritsail would be furled. The helmsman would put the tiller hard down, and the great main yard would swing around the mast.

"Leave go and haul!" Master Jones would cry, and the crewmen would release the lines so that the sails brought the ship onto its new heading. Then everyone would grab the lines and help haul until the mainsail was held fast to its new station.

It was hard, sometimes backbreaking work, but we were all glad of it. Our muscles grew slack from disuse, and the labor gave us another thing to concern ourselves with. It was most discouraging to think only of the miserable conditions below.

I grew quite handy with sails and lines, and Father allowed himself a rare word of praise.

"This will stand you well when we are in our new home," he told me. "There we will have need of seamanship; much promise is held out for the fortune to be made from fishing the American coast."

Thereafter, I endeavored to learn even more. When the winds grew intense, I would join the sailors in clewing the sails, or lending slack to avoid tears. I also learned to furl the topsails, a bit of a challenge as it involved standing on the swaying main yard, rolling the sail tight against the mainsail yard, and fastening it in place with a short line known as a gasket. Once I nearly fell overboard.

During storms, no passengers were allowed aloft, however. As the winds howled with the devil's own fury, Master Jones would order the ship hulled. Every stitch of sail would be furled. The ship would then ride out the storm. Sometimes we would be pitched fore and aft like a bit of cork bobbing on a lake. But

Mayflower was always worthy of her task, and we emerged from each tempest a bit battered but still intact.

No matter how many storms we endured, it was never possible to ignore the danger. John Howland, a servant of Master Samuel Fuller, nearly lost his life when wind and sea combined to pitch him over the side of the ship. The man was most fortunate, for he managed to grab a tops'l halyard and cry out.

We rushed to the ship's side to see a bit of a man's boot breaking the waves. Two sailors grabbed the halyard and announced that John must be holding on yet, for there was something at the free end. The men pulled together, hauling furiously in spite of the great chill which took possession of their wrists and arms. As I watched, icy air filled my lungs so that I thought I could breathe no more. Even so, I remained at hand until poor John was brought back from the sea even as Jonah had been purged by the whale. Much thanksgiving followed his rescue.

There was other news to celebrate as well. God blessed Master Stephen Hopkins and his wife Elizabeth with the birth of a son. They named him Oceanus, in honor of the voyage.

Soon after Oceanus was born, I fell under the watchful eye of Master Clarke, the first mate. Each day he would glance up as Edward and I climbed the rigging. One day he drew me aside and asked my name.

"Richard Woodley," I said rather more proudly than Father might have wished.

"And are you one of these Saints then, boy?" the mate inquired.

"Yes, sir," I replied. "Bound for the Americas."

"Ye've a lively step in the rigging, son. Have you learned your knots?"

I told him I had, and he asked me to show him a sheet bend. In the wink of an eye, I had sheet and line joined.

"Well, ye can take pride in a sailor's craft," Master Clarke declared as he matched my knot in half the time. "And if the tobacco fields prove too taxing for your spirit, I suspect we can always find a berth for you aboard *Mayflower*."

Thereafter he greeted me daily. Sometimes he would take Edward and me aside and show us a chart of the Virginia coast. Other times he would tell of his wanderings to the Indies or north where fish as big as Thom could be pulled from the ocean. Best of all, though, he invited me to take a turn at steering the ship.

"Do not show reluctance, Richard," Master Clarke bade me. "There are no rocks for you to run us against, and young Derry, the helmsman, stands ready should you grow weak."

"Aye, sir," I said, following Master Clarke to the steerage. There I was showed the whipstaff, a vertical beam the width of a rowing oar. My hands closed on the staff.

"Hold it steady lest I command otherwise," Master Clarke told me. Then he left the cabin for his post on the poop deck.

It was a strange sensation, feeling the power of the sea and the weight of *Mayflower* in my hands. I kept the staff as near still as was possible.

"Starboard a little," Master Clarke called down through the open hatch overhead.

"Here, lad, let her go a bit left," Derry said, showing me how to ease the staff over. "If ye wish to go starboard, let the staff swing a bit portside. If ye wish her bound over port, then let the staff slide starboard."

I nodded my understanding.

"Steady now!" Master Clarke called down.

"Move her back to center, lad," Derry told me. "Nary a trace o' nerves in ye. Aye, you've the makings of a seaman, that's assured."

I grew used to Master Clarke's voice and Derry's instructions, and before long, I was steering the ship as if born to the task.

"Full and by," the mate might order, or "Keep her off."

I would push the staff hard over or ease it back as commanded.

"If ever you tire of sainthood, Richard Woodley," Master Clarke said afterward as he led me back to the main deck, "send word to John Clarke that he's got himself a mate to train."

I confess it was a notion that had not a little appeal to it. Life aboard ship, with its adventures and dangers, made the labors of a farmer pale.

Our one great calamity struck us soon afterward. One of the main beams, a great thwart-ship timber, cracked from the strain of the ship's weighty cargo and the rigors of the stormy passage. It was a grave concern to all, since water rained down upon the pas-

sengers, compounding their misery. It also wetted the
cargo and drove the ship to an ever deeper draft. Mr.
Jones kept men at the pumps day and night, but they
scarcely could keep pace with the flooding. All our
company, myself included, looked on with alarm as
Mayflower struggled to make progress.

All was far from lost, though. Among those aboard
was a man especially skilled in carpentry, one Elias
Story by name. Among our cargo was a great screw
which we had brought with us to aid in the erection
of houses. Elias Story applied the screw to the weak-
ened beam, then braced the deck with other timber.
The crew caulked the deck, and the danger was averted.

"The Lord provides challenges, but He also supplies
aid," Elder Brewster told us the following Sabbath.
Even some of the more profane among the crew remarked that surely God must have His eye upon us.

I do not know which among us first sighted land.
In the middle of our tenth week at sea, snow white
gulls began to flock around the ship. Some of the sailors tossed out hooks in hope of catching cod or other
fresh fish, but they had little success. Another two
days' sailing drew us close to a broad stretch of white
beach.

"It does not appear to be Virginia," Master Clarke
pronounced. "Nor are we near the Hudson. I judge us
to be far north."

Mr. Coppin agreed, and Master Jones took out his
charts. The elders met and discussed a course of action. For a time we attempted to run southward, but

dangerous shoals interrupted our path. Instead we turned back to the north and made our way along the coast, searching out a suitable harbor.

"Will we be landing soon?" we all asked. "When can we step ashore?"

But there were few answers. Some fretted over the seemingly hostile landscape before us—only great rolling dunes of sand, studded with strange trees and shrubbery. No signs of life appeared, neither civilized nor savage.

"This land is more barren than the Netherlands," Mary said bitterly as I stood beside her glancing at the distant beach. "There are no trees. Where are the hills?"

I knew not, and though I tried to comfort her with tales I had heard from the mates, she was clearly discouraged. Mother complained bitterly that we had been deceived.

"It's the king's doing," she told us. "He means to cast us off on this foreign shore and leave us to perish."

"Master Jones will find us a harbor," I said.

"Yes," Father added. "What if we are not in Virginia? Were not we worried at the treatment we might receive at the hands of our countrymen? Here perhaps we might fashion our own colony, a new and better place than any yet known."

The words cheered all who heard them, and afterward Father spoke them again and again to the disheartened among our company.

Worse news was soon to come, though. Young William Butten, a servant of Master Samuel Fuller, took fever and died. For the company to suffer such a loss as we approached land was bitter indeed. William

Butten was nigh the age of John Alden, and we prayed this would be enough loss for the present.

Master Jones finally located a good sheltered harbor on the inland shore of a place that Master Clarke called Cape Cod. There was much fishing to be had, and I sat with Edward in the rigging and watched great whales bounding in the sea nearby. If we had proper boats and lances, Master Clarke said we could make much profit by killing these great fish for the oil contained in their flesh. But as we were after a place to settle, we set about the business of finding a proper spot.

"Praise God we are delivered out of a great wilderness," Father said as he brought Mother and Mary and little Thom to the main deck. "Surely a bountiful future lies before us in this new land."

But as I stared at the barren beaches before us, I saw no sign of bounty. It appeared a most hostile land, with no friend to welcome us and no harvest to sustain us through winter. It was already November, and the icy wind crept through my cloak so that I shivered. I prayed Father was right, but our years in Leyden had taught me that life mostly offered hardship and disappointment. I remembered *Speedwell* and Thomas back in England, and I prepared myself for the trials ahead.

THREE
LAND

It was most difficult to remain aboard ship with the shoreline so near. Mother and the other women especially displayed a great eagerness to touch solid ground. Captain Standish wished to explore the distant shore as soon as was practical, and Father agreed. But there were many delays. *Mayflower* could approach no closer than a few hundred yards. Her deep draft, which had served us so well in heavy seas, now prevented us from entering the shallows. She would remain at anchor offshore.

Having foreseen the need to travel by sea upon landing, the elders had carried amidst the cargo a shallop, a long boat that could be equipped with sail. The vessel was ideal for carrying small parties of men up rivers or along the shore. Many such boats were employed in the fishing trade.

Our own shallop was ill-suited for immediate use, having been poorly stowed so that sweating casks and leaking seawater had damaged it during our long voyage. *Mayflower*'s carpenters, assisted by skilled passengers, set about making repairs because we preferred to use our shallop instead of the ship's small boats.

Meanwhile, our company was faced with a more serious problem. Discovering that we were rather far north of the Virginia colony, many of the Strangers asserted they were no longer bound by such agreements as they had made before boarding ship.

Unlike the members of the Leyden congregation who desired to retain a sense of community, these Strangers sought only the opportunity to attain land and build their futures. Elder Brewster, Mr. William Bradford, and others spoke for unity, however. Amongst us there were but fifty men, and ahead of us lay an untamed wilderness possessed of a savage and possibly hostile population. Spring was long past, and already the chill winds of winter whined through *Mayflower*'s rigging. Food supplies would be stretched at best, and we had no shelter.

Moreover, Master Christopher Martin, chosen by the merchant adventurers to govern us on our voyage, had lost the respect of the company. He made little effort to maintain order. Aboard ship there had been but few problems. Now men argued violently, and open warfare threatened to explode.

So, what was to be done? Would our company, after such trials in England, with *Speedwell*, and after sixty-six days at sea, find itself undone by a handful of malcontents even as we readied ourselves to set foot on the American continent?

Events got no better. Master Jones, while sympathetic, had little desire to stay forever at anchor off Cape Cod. Some among the crew were for unloading us and our supplies and beating a fast course back to England.

Father told me Elder Brewster first struck upon the idea of the compact. Master Bradford, being also gifted with words, helped in its drafting. After much discussion, a document was drawn up.

When preparations were complete, a meeting was called of the company. More than ninety of us huddled together on the windswept deck of *Mayflower* as Elder Brewster read the words to all.

In the Name of God, Amen.

> We whose names are underwritten, the loyal subjects of our dread Sovereign Lord King James, by the Grace of God of Great Britain, France, and Ireland King, Defender of the Faith, etc.
> Having undertaken, for the Glory of God and advancement of the Christian Faith and Honour of our King and Country, a Voyage to plant the First Colony in the Northern Parts of Virginia, do by these presents solemnly and mutually in the presence of God and of one another, Covenant and Combine ourselves together into a Civil Body Politic, for our better ordering and preservation and furtherance of the ends aforesaid, and by virtue hereof to enact, constitute and frame such just and equal Laws, Ordinances, Acts, Constitutions, and Offices, from time to time, as shall be thought most meet and convenient for the general good of the Colony, unto which we promise all due submission and obedience. In witness whereof we have hereunder subscribed our names at Cape Cod, the 11th of November, in the year of the reign of our Sovereign Lord King James, of England, France, and Ireland the eighteenth, and of Scotland the fifty-fourth. Anno Domini 1620.

When the elder had finished his reading, a pen was made ready. Each man stepped forward in turn to affix his name.

Shortly thereafter an election was held to select our first governor. Many names were put forth, but the company finally settled upon Master John Carver, an elderly merchant known and liked by all. Master Carver drew the company together, and soon even the harshness of the weather failed to dim our renewed hope.

There remained a restlessness among us to venture forth, though. For myself, I'd grown accustomed to the feel of a rolling deck, but dreams of adventure ashore beckoned to my very soul. There is an impatience that comes of being twelve, and my feet could scarcely be constrained from setting forth on their own.

After passing the Sabbath in prayer, we collected ourselves on *Mayflower*'s main deck Monday morning. At last the call had come to go ashore. Even now, the carpenters had not yet readied the shallop, but it was no longer possible to put off the company. Mother, Mary, and other women gathered all manner of clothing and linens to be washed, and men collected hatchets and saws for the cutting of wood. Small numbers of the company were then rowed ashore by sailors in the ship's boats. Even so, the passengers were forced to wade the final hundred yards through the freezing water, for the heavily laden boats would venture no closer for fear of grounding.

I stood with the other children and watched as the first men waded to the beach. Some fell upon their knees and gave thanks. After a brief exploration was made of the area, women were also brought across the shallows to land. I looked longingly as Mother and Mary began scrubbing our clothing.

"I never knew English children to stand clear when there was work to be done," Master Clarke said to us. "Have ye never heard there are fish to be caught? Why, many's the time I've dug a goodly number of mussels and clams on shore."

His words had the effect of stirring us to action.

"Can we not go?" Edward asked as others flocked to the boats. "Thom is in the care of Elizabeth Tilley. Look to the others."

I certainly intended to go myself, for Father had spoken no command to the contrary. So, with Edward at my side, I joined the other children who were thought up to the hazards of the landing and climbed into one of the longboats.

From *Mayflower*'s deck, the journey from ship to shore had appeared a simple prospect. But when the sailors helped us into the shallows, it became quite a test for us. My feet sank into the sandy bottom, and water splashed at my neck. The smaller ones had it far worse. Those of us who were taller had to pull the others along by hand or shoulder. I wrapped my fingers around Edward's wrist and did my best to help him along. It was not easy. A harsh wind blew spray into my eyes, and the cold made my legs feel like stone. I arrived at the beach shivering from head to foot.

Edward was already coughing, and I was very glad of a fire built by the woodcutters. Mary left the washing long enough to help us out of our damp jerkins. We shed our soaked boots and waterlogged stockings and tried as best we could to shake the water out of our hair.

"Father will not be pleased that Edward came," Mary scolded as she draped a woolen blanket over our shoulders. "He will have words for you, I fear."

I frowned. She was, no doubt, correct. There were times when I considered brothers grievous afflictions.

Father, being occupied with the other woodcutters, had no immediate words for me, however. Edward and I shook ourselves as free from water as we could while waiting for our clothes to dry. Afterward, we joined the other boys along the beach.

We were occupied the remainder of the day digging in the soft sand with our hands for clams and mussels. We located a great number. Their shells were as big as my hands. Inside were shiny stones the sailors called sea pearls.

As night fell, the sailors ferried us back to the ship. The company seemed renewed by the day's labors. Our wood supply was replenished, and our clothes had been laundered.

My own efforts proved less successful. Edward continued his coughing, and Father spoke strongly to me for allowing him to come ashore. I did not deem myself responsible for my brother, but neither did I voice my opinion. It only would have brought hours of Scripture to read. I was glad the rod was spared for once.

Our mussels were eaten with great enthusiasm, but later most of the company took ill and cast them up. Even the sailors became sick, and it was thought perhaps winter was not their season. For my own part, I spent half that night with my head over the side of the ship, and I have had little hunger for mussels since.

Each day thereafter parties visited the shore. It seemed that after months at sea, there was no end to the washing. More wood was cut so that we could keep our fires burning. The men busied themselves hunting the ducks and other fowl which seemed to cover the shoreline. We had occasion to bless much good food.

The elders worried over a sight for our permanent habitation, and with the shallop as yet not repaired, it was decided that Captain Standish would lead a party of sixteen well-armed men ashore. An exploration might then be made of the shoreline, following what appeared to be the mouth of a river or a small inlet.

Captain Standish's party set forth on Wednesday. Each man wore his corselet and carried both sword and musket. I followed their progress as best I could from *Mayflower*. They proceeded along the beach in single file a mile or more. Then they entered the woodland and vanished from sight.

The company waited anxiously for Captain Standish and his fellow explorers to return. The shadows we saw at dawn quickly became bands of armed savages. With a third of the men away, the distance from shore, which had seemed so great when we were wading through the shallows, appeared to be nothing at all.

Soon I had little time to concern myself with Captain Standish. Edward worsened, and Father, declaring I was responsible, decided I should keep watch over Edward's illness. Mary found an extra blanket, and I fed my brother a broth Mother had made from a duck breast.

"I feel as though I might die," Edward told me after drinking it.

"Mother says you shall not die," I said, covering his ears with one of Mary's old stockings. "She has had the women hard at work, down upon their knees reading verse and praying. I fear you will be sorely obligated to all of them for many years."

"Perhaps I would be better buried," Edward said. I saw in his eyes the old brightness and knew nothing ill would come of the coughing, other than much worry on my part that I should be held accountable for the death of a brother.

As Edward was at last able to sit up without growing faint, I summoned Thom and shared some of the tales I had heard earlier from the mates. Master Clarke himself joined us upon occasion, telling terrifying stories of the five years he was held by the Spanish. Such captivity, with its accompanying tortures, was enough to persuade me that life in Leyden had been as a paradise.

"And yet you still set off to sea?" I asked.

"Aye, 'tis the only life for a restless soul," Master Clarke told us. "There're worse fates than running upon a rock or being cast into a sea."

"But it's scarcely left you time to begin a family," Mary said, appearing like a spectre from out of the darkness. "Surely you must miss your family."

"Oh, I've my ship for a mother, a master for a father,

and who was ever without brothers who sailed with such mates as mine?"

Still it didn't seem the same as a family, and I was glad of the knowledge that Mother was there to tend us and cook and that Father's strong shoulders took the measure of each task. Mary stood ever ready to purge my soul, and Edward and Thom let me know I was needed.

Captain Standish returned after two days of exploration. He gave vivid accounts of half-naked savages and told of finding great mounds of earth filled with the bones of the dead. Other mounds contained great heaps of hard Indian corn, which the captain had brought back to serve us as seed when the time for planting arrived.

The explorers brought back a large iron kettle likely traded off a ship or else salvaged from a wreck. Bows, arrows, and other weapons had been found in the mounds. Out of reverence for the dead, all items save the kettle and the corn had been returned to the earth.

I wished to hear more from Captain Standish and the others, but my time was scarce. And after ten days passed, the captain set out once more, this time accompanied by a score of men.

They returned shortly with more corn, but they had failed to locate and treat with any savages. Nor had they found a suitable place for our habitation. December was now hard upon us, and twice winter storms bade us welcome with a blanket of snow.

During this time a second child was born. Mrs. Susanna White, wife of Master William White, a wool-carder devoted to our cause, brought into our midst a boy who was named Peregrine. The child's older brother, Resolved, who was the same age as my brother Thom, stayed most of this time with us. Mistress White, lacking female servants, borrowed Mary for a time to help with the baby.

Edward and I were less than delighted with this turn. Mother bestowed upon us those duties Mary normally tended, and we were not relieved of any of our own. The preparation of food was especially irksome, and the other boys aboard *Mayflower* delighted in fixing on us the most uncomplimentary titles.

The third exploration was by far the most eventful. By now the shallop had been readied. Consequently Captain Standish took most of the fittest men in the company, together with two seamen from the ship's company and Master Clarke and Master Coppin, the master gunner. The party was split. Captain Standish led seven men by land. The others traveled by sea in the shallop. They were gone a grievous long while, and while fresh storms found us nightly, we worried over them. The captain and his men had set out into hostile land with little more than the clothes on their backs for warmth.

All returned in time, and Captain Standish related a most extraordinary adventure. For the first time our men had actually encountered savages.

"It was a most severe engagement," Master Clarke told Edward, me, and the other boys who huddled in a corner of the steerage cabin that night. "Many of us had hung our clothing in the trees. These savages, mistaking our garments for ourselves, shot many arrows. My own shirt was pierced three times."

The mate showed us the holes in his shirt, then revealed an arrow he had carried from the battle as a remembrance.

"Arrows rained down upon us. We little knew what course to pursue. Captain Standish ordered his men to return fire, and the muskets barked. All save one of the savages raced off. This one, a most stately man, shouted in his accursed tongue words which we took to be all manner of insult. Finally a musket shot found the branch near his head, and this last savage followed his fellows.

"We gave chase for a time, but it was not thought prudent to pursue. Afterward we collected eighteen arrows, though many more were shot at us. Although we visited some dwellings of these Indians, we caught no further sight of life."

After Master Clarke's story, I dreamed of little other than the savages. I always found myself bravely defeating the enemy with my few companions.

Following this third exploration, the elders met to talk about the site of our plantation. Cape Cod was considered unsuitable. There were no fields free of timber, and the natives were clearly hostile. The earth was sandy, poorly suited to farming. Yet we stood at anchor in the best harbor. None better was known.

The crew, however, spoke of a more promising place not far distant. Years before it had been the sight of much stealing from the Indians, hence it was known thereafter as Thievish Harbor. Narrow banks of earth formed a barrier to the current, making it possible for a ship to safely ride out every gale.

"We must seek out this place," the men decided. And so the shallop was loaded with appropriate men and supplies for the quest.

The company pitted much hope on the outcome of the shallop's voyage. Many hours were passed in prayer and meditation for the explorers. We no longer found warmth anywhere aboard ship, and each of us feared the peril that awaited in the wild and hostile country.

The earlier explorations were nothing compared to this fourth one. The shallop set off and was quickly lost to view. Our imaginations filled with scenes of terrible butchery, torture, and grave sickness. Despair began to spread among the passengers.

Harsh winds now painted *Mayflower's* deck and rigging with ice. The moans and coughs of the sick never ended. I thanked God that Edward was restored to health, and we held Thom close through the night, for his small body trembled fearfully from the cold.

Others were less fortunate. Edward Thompson, a servant of Master White, breathed his last the fourth day of December. Two days hence a sadder death followed. Jasper More, a boy in the service of Governor Carver, fell ill of the cold and never regained his strength.

Death continued to stalk the decks of *Mayflower.* Young Dorothy Bradford, only three and twenty years of age, fell from the ship and was lost. Some were quick to say she jumped. Her young son, John, had been left in the Netherlands, and her husband, Master

William Bradford, was away in the shallop. All mourned for Mistress Dorothy, and many a tear was shed.

"What victory can death win over our stout hearts?" Father asked as we gathered that evening around our meager dinner. "We are strong. We will build our new home soon."

But James Chilton followed Dorothy Bradford, and as the days passed without news of the shallop, what hopes remained grew dimmer and dimmer until there was scarce hope to be found throughout the company.

"What could have befallen them?" I asked Father one night as the snows fell again upon us. "Can they be lost?"

"Not so long as God looks to their souls," Father said, touching my shoulder lightly in a manner he had not practiced in many months. "We, too, will continue to be blessed while we profess ourselves one with God's laws."

It was not always easy to conduct oneself each day according to Scripture, but I endeavored to do my utmost. And when finally the shallop's slight silhouette was spotted, it occasioned a great thanksgiving by the company and crew alike. We waited anxiously to learn the results of their journey.

FOUR

THIEVISH HARBOR

When the explorers boarded *Mayflower*, they first enjoyed a reunion with their families. It was a time of joy for most. Although for Master Bradford, there was the sad news of Mistress Dorothy's drowning.

After all were fed and warm clothes were exchanged for those coated with sea spray, the men in our company gathered to hear the reports of the explorers. I had to content myself with waiting for Father to relate their story toward nightfall.

All manner of calamity had befallen the shallop. Early on, she broke her rudder, so the crew was forced to steer using two oars. Later, the mast had splintered in three places, and the sail had been lost overboard. But despite great difficulties, they located a fair anchorage. Going ashore, they found much cleared land, bounded by a brook of clear, sweet water. There were great woods nearby to supply timber for houses.

After some brief discourse, Master Jones weighed anchor. Not long after, favorable winds carried *Mayflower* to within sight of a broad harbor which rested between two narrow spits of land.

"Aye, 'tis Thievish Harbor, fairly enough," Master Clarke told me as I searched the distant shore for some sign of life. "I've put in here afore."

Master Coppin nodded his head in agreement.

Master Jones then put the crew to the difficult task of bringing the ship into harbor. *Mayflower* made a half circle and briefly closed with the land. The winds played a most devilish game with the ship's sails, though, and we were cast out as toward the open sea. It was nightfall before *Mayflower* again sighted Thievish Harbor.

The next morn Master Jones made another attempt to bring the ship within the harbor. He sent the mates forward and began shouting the steerage commands. I, being on the poop deck, could hear the helmsman swearing heavily as he leaned hard against the whipstaff.

"All hands on deck!" Master Clarke cried out.

Perhaps two dozen of our company joined the crew in swinging the mainsail and topsail yards around. *Mayflower* responded with another half turn. Before the lines could be secured, Mr. Jones brought the ship about. The sailors furled the topsail, and the ship made its way slowly around a sandbar and into the harbor.

The crew gave a shout, then busied themselves sounding the ocean lest *Mayflower* run aground. Master Jones dropped anchor a quarter league offshore. That day being Saturday, and the hour late as well, it was decided we should occupy ourselves with preparations for the Sabbath and put off our landing until Monday.

Delaying our landing such a long time was most difficult. Winter winds kept the ship constantly in motion, and many had taken chills from their long hours on deck exposed to the cold of the season. The Sabbath was especially trying for young ones like me.

We were less than attentive to the words of the elders, and not a few of us received from the rod a lesson in the merits of listening.

Monday an exploration was made of the beach, which we now called Plymouth. Master Jones said it was so named by an English captain, John Smith, some six years past.

"It is an apt name for the place," Father declared. "In Plymouth we bade farewell to our trials in England, and it is best not to choose the name of a pirate harbor."

In the days that followed, we found Plymouth to be a wondrous place indeed. The harbor was large and well sheltered, if at times difficult to enter. There were broad fields near the beach and a fine, free-flowing brook. Inland lay vast woodlands filled with tall, straight trees, and much plant life we were little acquainted with.

The town site appeared to have been inhabited by savages not long before, but we saw no signs that any dwelt there presently. It was a great mystery as to what had become of them, and it was a constant terror that they might return in force.

The soil was rich and black. Father, who said it put him in mind of Yorkshire, boasted that the fields would grow tall with wheat and barley. There were many hills once planted with Indian corn, and we hoped to put our seed to good purpose. A few poles and frames of what must have been primitive huts stood near the fields.

We located all manner of clay and stone. Much of it was soft and quite suitable for the making of pottery.

We also drank water from the brook and found it greatly to our liking. We replenished the ship's water casks.

"Was there ever so sweet a taste?" Father asked.

I confessed that I had never partaken of better, and I deemed it a fine omen for our future in the Americas.

The trees promised to be not only a rich source for building homes and furniture, but also for the keels and masts of future ships.

As the close of December neared, the weather worsened. Mr. Jones set three anchors in the ocean bottom so that *Mayflower* might rest as secure as possible. Though most of the men worked ashore in the daylight hours, it was not thought safe as yet for them to remain after dusk. Captain Standish was quick to remind the company of the inhospitable savages on Cape Cod, and he warned against the threat of attack.

Of equal concern was the harsh nature of the weather. The cruel wind and the bitter cold began to sap our strength. Goodwife Allerton was delivered of a son on the twenty-second day of December, but the child proved to be stillborn. It was the first mischance of birth since our departure from Leyden, and we were all overcome with sadness. Mother and the other women made great efforts to console Goody Allerton, but God indeed places a heavy burden when He warrants the death of a child. I recalled the sorrow that draped our house when my sister Susanna was taken from us.

Despite our grief, the very next day the shoreline rang with the sound of axes felling tall timbers. While such work was beyond us, Edward and I aided in stripping the bark and doing what we could manage with saws. It was frightfully cold, and Edward took chill rapidly when our work was completed. I felt certain Father would soon order him confined to ship.

The twenty-fourth being a Sabbath, those of our company who could be put ashore collected themselves for the reading of the Scripture. Many of the Strangers kept to themselves, preparing for the celebration of Christmas. They believed that the twenty-fifth marked the day of our Savior's birth and thus celebrated it. Elder Brewster maintained that there was no proof of the fact, for the Scriptures name no such date. Though the Strangers prepared for much merriment, Father said we must continue with our labors as befitted God-fearing people.

Our reverence was disturbed not by the Strangers, however, but by a loud cry from the distant wood. Captain Standish immediately formed the men, but whatever the noise, it was not the command for a general attack upon us as was most feared. The men searched the wood but discovered nothing. We were much relieved and made great our thanks for God's deliverance. I confess I was quite grateful when we returned to the ship.

With the coming of Monday, we set to work constructing a common house. Although few of the Strangers joined us in our efforts, since they were observing their festivities, we made good progress. Soon foundation timbers were cut, rived, and blocked as might have been done in Dorset or Kent. Joiners made each plank secure by inserting narrow pegs into notches in the timbers.

With others devoted to the sawing, I aided a group of boys who were gathering thatch for the roof. The brook and small ponds nearby abounded in rushes, and molding a thatch, though tedious work, presented no great problems. The women, when not tending the smaller children or doing the cooking, helped in our work. I must admit that Mary was better suited to the work, for my hands betrayed me more than once as I wove rush and grass.

Our new home lay in a most damp country, and it seemed we were forever wet. The sailors who brought us ashore in the ship's boats each day took no particular care to insure we reached land, and many of us were cast into a sea that was well over our heads. The ground where we worked was half bog, and our boots were inadequate defense against the dampness. More days than not were marred by rain.

Great fires were kept burning ashore to provide warmth, but nothing abated the chills that swept *Mayflower*. Worse, supplies of everything dwindled. The entire company greeted most sadly the news that the last of the beer had been drunk. It was but another reminder that we were no longer part of Mother England.

We were unable to reach shore at all some days on account of terrible rain squalls which tossed *Mayflower* about and made us miserable. There was no hope of rowing ashore in such conditions.

"What will come of us if this weather persists?" Mother asked as our family crowded together in the narrow bunk she and Father had shared throughout our voyage. The deck was wet, and it was thought unfit even for us boys to occupy.

"God will send us fair weather soon," Father assured her. "We will pass from this trial as we have all others."

But Mother was clearly worried. Edward was rarely without his cough, and young Thom had grown pale and weary. He wanted color in his cheeks. I awoke once to see him sitting beside me more death than brother. Of us all, only Mary maintained her spirits. She would rest Thom on her lap and sing to him. She kept Edward in dry shirts and myself out of mischief.

"I hope when my time comes to be a wife and mother God shall bless me with daughters," she often re-marked. "Boys are almost always underfoot and good for little as I can see."

It might be thought that with so many other trials before us Father would have excused Edward and me from our study, but such was not the case. True we read more from Job and Daniel since the cold had come, but he put us to our Aristotle as well.

"An educated man may rise to high station in a land such as this," Father said. "You may perhaps set your-self up as an equal to young William Bradford or even Elder Brewster. A man may forfeit wealth or property, but he always carries with him the knowledge he has digested."

I wished more than once that he had used some other word, for I was perpetually famished aboard ship. The storms kept our men from pursuing water-fowl with their muskets, and the day salt horse had carried a flavor was long past. Provisions were quite low, and Master Jones kept back what his crew would need in recrossing the Atlantic.

I was delighted when we returned to our labors. My arms had grown stiff from disuse, and I was weary of being crowded below deck. I was allowed to aid Father in joining the great timbers which would frame the roof and ceiling. I held the pegs as he hammered them into the timbers.

This was no mean employ. I was forced to balance myself on a narrow beam as I practiced my craft. Later, when the roof timbers were in place, I aided in weaving the thatch.

The building which took shape was not as big as the hall of our home in Leyden, being little more than a pole squared. A pole being roughly equal to a rod, each wall stretched some five and a half yards. Still, it looked most impressive in that barren land, and we all took great pride in its grandeur. But the timbers were almost no shield from the whining December winds, and the cold, damp floor lacked the cover of deep straw or rugs.

With walls of wattle and daub, it resembled a poor tenant farmer's house. Wattle was normally used in building chicken coops or pig styes, but we availed ourselves of it, knowing how precious time was.

With great progress being made on the common house, it was decided by the elders that the time had come for laying out the village. Towns in Europe were traditionally laid out either in circles or squares. The oldest cities were once enclosed by great walls and parapets. With the threat of attack from savages ever present, it was thought fitting to design our town as a fortress as much as a habitation. All land was to be held in common our first seven years, so there was need of keeping the community near.

The plan drawn up called for only two streets, meeting in a cross near the midoint of the village. The town would occupy a small hill on the north bank of what had now been named Town Brook and reach to the beach. Land was allotted to each of the nineteen families in our company. Single men were asked to join families, lest we need too many structures.

The single men were glad of this arrangement. In a harsh and desolate country, they were thankful to have someone offer them companionship and a warm dinner. To each person in a family, regardless of age or stature, a property half a pole in breadth and three in length was assigned. So it was that our allotment was eighteen poles deep and three in breadth. There would be adequate space for house, stockyard, and garden.

Locations were drawn by lot. Our own land would rest alongside that of Mr. Edward Winslow, whose holdings were smaller because, though he had servants, he had no children.

The houses which grew upon these lots were little more than huts. Some were no better than a Walloon farmer would devote to his goose. Still, they offered some scant shelter against the elements. Taking into account the growing weakness of the people, many of whom were ill with grave coughs and great chills, perhaps such huts were as much as could be properly expected.

On days of rain, little was accomplished. More than once I wondered if I would ever again feel dry. I occupied most of my Sabbath prayers with pleas for fair weather or better prospects.

For lack of deep water, *Mayflower* continued to stand offshore. Much time was spent in bringing men ashore at dawn and taking them back aboard at dusk. But until shelter was finished in our little town, there was no safe place for workers to abide.

January arrived, and the cold grew even worse. Even so, we kept at our tasks. One morning while I was gathering thatch with Mary, I smelled smoke from not far away. Others joined us, pointing to a light white cloud curling skyward from where the Indian village had stood.

Consequently, Captain Standish ordered four of our men to arm themselves and stand ready to defend the town. Women and children were taken to safety, but no savages appeared. The next day a spirited group set out in search of the elusive natives. But although the captain and his companions scoured the woods and searched the abandoned village, they failed to catch so much as a glimpse of an Indian.

Captain Standish did demonstrate his marksmanship by shooting a large eagle. Those who partook of the roasted bird found the meat to be most excellent, not unlike mutton in taste. Since eagles frequented the upper heavens, we had few opportunities to discover for ourselves the merits of eagle meat, however.

Next day one of the sailors discovered a large herring on the beach. Master Jones of *Mayflower* enjoyed the herring for dinner, and our company was put in hope of fine fishing. Save one cod, we had nary a

minnow for all our efforts. The sailors judged the fault
to lie with our hooks, which were said to be too large
for capturing the fish which swam the brook or inhabited the shallow coastal waters.

Our hardships were only beginning. Soon we were
fortunate when we could work for more than a few
hours of each day. Our parties returned to *Mayflower*
weary and damp from the rain and cold.

I abandoned all hope of ever being warm again. The
great quantities of wood we brought from shore had
little effect against the brutal American winter.

Now began a time of great hunger, too. The elders
had set great store in the tales of fishing spread by
sailors, but other than occasional fowl, we were forced
to rely on our meager stores brought from Southampton. I watched in sadness as the eyes of my mother
and brothers grew dim. Father turned to Scripture for
comfort. I found only the most severe labors cast the
cold and hunger from my mind.

Master Christopher Martin took to his sickbed that
first week of the new year. Master Martin had been
entrusted with the accounts by the merchants, and
many of our shortages were thought due to mishan-
dling. He spoke with a harshness of tongue and had
never been popular among the company. We Saints
had been especially displeased by his bearing, as he
was continually ordering about his fellows. Even so,
we would not have wished him ill. His stepson, young
Solomon Prower, had gone to his maker earlier, and
it was thought by most that God's punishment had
already befallen the Martin family.

Governor Carver met with Master Martin. The accounts were found to be in such disorder as to be almost entirely useless. Amidst a great deal of grumbling and little sorrow Master Martin coughed out his life.

Mid-January provided a brief break in the dismal weather. At first light, the sailors rowed every able-bodied man ashore to work on the common house. Men were given leave to labor on their own houses as well, the thought being that the work might be hastened on those smaller dwellings.

Soon the common house lacked only thatch for its roof, and two rows of houses stood in varying degrees of completion. Father and I constructed from turf and branches a small roundish hut. It kept little wind out, but it was the first true home I had ever known.

"This we have built with our own hands, Richard," Father announced proudly. I could hear the weariness in his voice, but his eyes shone like stars on a dark December eve.

"Yes," I said, clasping his hand. But later when we huddled together in the berth on *Mayflower*, I did not see the same glow in Edward's eyes. Little Thom scarce understood our words. Only Mary and Mother continued as before. I supposed their constant labors kept the hunger and cold at bay.

The days that followed were the worst of the season. By noon we were subjected to heavy rains, which by nightfall would change to ice. Great blizzards of snow would come by morning. We considered ourselves most fortunate to work three days each week.

On one storm-plagued morning, a great wave upset our boat as we approached the beach. I found myself pitched into a rolling sea. For a brief time I thought myself drowned, but one of the sailors dragged me ashore. I shivered from the cold, and breathing the frigid air sent icy spears into my lungs. I wished to be of help to Father, but I could barely stand. Sailors bore me to the common house and set me beside a blazing fire. My clothes were removed and I was covered by a blanket of coarse wool. Later I was ferried back to *Mayflower* where I fell into a great slumber.

FIVE
THE GREAT SICKNESS

I passed into my thirteenth year during that great sleep. My eyes failed to greet the daylight for the better part of a week. During that time my mind clouded with a thousand thoughts, mostly visions of a terrible judgment which held me accountable for all manner of misdeeds I had committed.

There was also the face of my old friend Thomas Cushman.

"You were wise to stay in England, Thomas," I told him. "We have found only death in this new land."

But it was not God's will that I should pass on into the night. I finally opened my eyes to discover I was lying in Mother's bunk aboard *Mayflower*. Mary stood beside me, attending my fevers.

"We feared you were upon a deathbed, Richard," she said, squeezing my palm.

"I . . . I fell overboard," I explained. "The sea was so cold."

"You were chilled to the bone," she told me. "Many prayers have been spoken for you these last five days."

"Five days?" I asked.

"You have been in God's hands all that time," Mary said, wiping my forehead with a warm cloth. "Mother has been most distraught. There have been more deaths. She takes it upon herself that you took the fever."

"How so?"

"She kept Edward aboard ship."

If I had been more alert I would have said something in reply. Often enough I had grumbled at what I considered my father's unfair expectations of me. But a great weariness possessed me, and I again slumbered.

For two more days I lay in bed, shivering from the cold and fighting to keep a bit of broth in my stomach. Mary and Mother sat dutifully at my side, tending my every need and praying for my recovery. Father continued his labors ashore.

Edward and Thom appeared from time to time, staring at me as if expecting I might die at any moment, and not wanting to miss such an event. Sometimes they would poke my side with their fingers or whisper my name to see if I remained alive. Once I frightened poor Thom halfway to his grave by closing my eyes, then suddenly rolling over so that his arm was trapped.

Thom stumbled away howling, and Mother rushed over to see what was afoot. Another time she might have laughed, but I noticed only a very weary relief spread across her exhausted face.

Mary was nearly as tired, but she at least would pass the night in peace. Mother was forever tending me or some other unfortunate among the company. Often I heard Stranger and Saint alike praise the name of Goody Woodley. I so wanted to rise from the bed and raise her spirits, but the strength eluded me.

"I fear him dying," Master Samuel Fuller, our physician, told Mother. "He is frightfully pale, and he seldom stirs."

"Nay, he's a strong lad," John Alden, the cooper,

declared. "A broken barrel needs time to mend. So it is with Richard."

I took the words to heart, and I fought to clear from my thoughts any notion of dying. The cold seemed to pass, and when a soft hand touched my chest, I cracked open my eyes.

"Lord Jehovah, spare this child of mine," Mother pleaded as she knelt beside me. I knew what was unspoken. She was remembering Susanna. Her eyes were ringed with circles, and her good and bountiful heart was surely cracking. I prayed for the strength to rise, and I prayed she might find some rest soon.

I surprised everyone that next morning by sitting up. Mother fed me a cup of broth and some hard biscuit, and by nightfall I was thought well enough to have Edward and Thom share my bunk.

"God must have taken your hand, Richard," Mary said, resting her hand on my shoulder.

I knew, looking into her tired eyes and those of my mother that He had not been the only one watching over me.

I grew stronger each day after, and soon I was able to help with the work once more. Mother would not allow me to go to the common house to aid Father with his labors, but there was much to be done aboard *Mayflower*. I began by assisting the ship's quartermaster with the handling of stores. But the casks which needed moving were beyond my strength, and I was of little use. Instead Master Clarke found employment for me caulking the ship's boats.

Ordinarily such duty would have been assigned to

the crew, but the sickness which plagued our company had not ignored the sailors. Many of those men were kept busy rowing parties from ship to shore, leaving them little time for other things. When Master Clarke asked if I might help, I recalled the many kindnesses he'd shown me while at sea. I remembered, too, that a sailor had pulled me from the sea. It seemed but little recompense.

I found caulking to my liking. It was not strenuous work, but it kept my hands employed. Master Clarke made a shelter of sorts out of a spare sail, and we worked underneath so that the wind and the cold were kept at bay. Edward and the Brewster boys joined in, and we even had young Thom helping with the sanding.

Later I would aid Mary in preparing our dinner, for Mother was beginning to show the strain of many sleepless nights. Her face was pale as the snow, and her eyes seemed drained of their rich blue color.

"I worry for her," Mary confessed. "She is forever tending others, but she will not suffer anyone to take her turn at the washing or the sewing."

"Yes," I admitted. "But work is the only shield against the cold. Had I lain another day in bed, I fear I would have frozen solid."

"Rest brought you back to us, Richard," Mary pronounced. "Lack of rest has carried many off in the night."

I nodded grimly and pledged to ease Mother's burdens.

For a few days Mother allowed Mary to take on the

washing. For my part, I helped Mistress Susanna White tend the sick sailors. Her brother, Master Samuel Fuller, ministered to the needs of the most severely ill aboard ship and also those sundry sick ashore. The ship's doctor, Mr. Giles Heape, was about also, bleeding the feverish and administering purges. Few among us placed any confidence in the violent treatments of the doctor. He had but scant success with his remedies, and more of his patients died than were made well.

The sailors were particularly miserable. They bled from the mouth, and several lost teeth.

"Aye, I've seen it afore, Richard," Master Clarke said. "Scurvy."

"Scurvy?"

" 'Tis common enough aboard ship. My father called it the bleeding sickness, and I've heard it comes with starving as well."

"What's to be done?"

"Give the men rest and such food as we have. It's as your people say, though. In God's hands."

The scurvy afflicted us all, but some suffered more than others. Older members of our company lost teeth, and a general infirmity possessed the women. Mother nearly fell cooking our dinner, but she would not hear of resting. The other women were much the same. They tended the sick, cooked the food, mended, and washed until they became too ill to stand.

The men roofed the common house. Thereafter, a great many remained ashore. Soon other huts were ready for habitation. Captain Standish sent men in search in fowl, and birds were shot. We had great need of food, and we rejoiced at the taste of stewed duck or baked goose. We now saw Father only on Sabbath when all of us gathered to ask the Lord's blessing.

"I thank God you came back to us, Richard," Father said when I greeted him aboard *Mayflower*. "My heart has been heavy this past week."

"I am sorry to have been such little help," I said. "I am growing stronger."

I could read in his tired eyes how frail I still was.

There were other signs as well. Even though I had grown slightly taller, my clothes hung so loose that Mother had to take in the waist of my breeches. I also noticed that the bones of my fingers nearly pierced the skin.

Edward and Thom were little better. Edward's face was pale and without its usual grin, while little Thom had taken to stumbling. I carried him on my shoulders whenever we had any distance to travel.

The other children were the same. When darkness fell, the *Mayflower* was awash with cries and moans. It had become a ship of women and children. The mates aided us in their own manner, but many of the crew held us accountable for their own maladies.

"We should be safe in Dartmouth Harbor," one young hand lamented. "I never thought my death'd find me ridin' anchor off Thievish Harbor in midwinter."

Among the seamen taken ill was the bosun. Although he had been both cruel and profane to us, the kindness of the women who tended him produced a change in his heart. He professed great gratitude and promised to mend his manners. But before he could demonstrate his Godliness, he passed on into the night.

The departure of the men and the depletion of the company left my brothers and me a bunk to ourselves. It offered some protection against the dampness of the 'tween decks area, but the air remained frigid. During storms seawater continued to pour down the hatches, dousing us all and bringing on spasms of cold.

Mother's face grew longer and longer.

"I do wish your father were here," she often remarked.

In his absence, she would lead us in simple prayers. Sometimes I would read from the Scriptures. Though I lacked Father's great knowledge of the Bible, I did find a few hopeful words in Matthew to share with my family.

As Mother grew less able to care for us, I took it upon myself to help Mary with the cooking. I had no talent for sewing, but I could watch a kettle. Captain Standish sent a goose from shore, and for a time spirits aboard *Mayflower* rose. But such spells of brightness never lingered.

Thom grew to be a special concern to me. He was so small, and though he never complained of hunger or cold, both seemed to grip him. At night I would pull him close so that I might share what warmth our bunk possessed. His feet were like ice, and his slight body shook throughout the night.

Edward spoke openly of his misery.

"Will I die of this fever?" he asked as I gave him his nightly broth.

"Am I a prophet?" I replied. "So long as others less pious live, I would not count myself among the doomed."

Thom asked no such questions. There was a sadness in his eyes that haunted me. At night I would see him searching my face for answers I did not possess. Often his thin fingers would grip my arm with a power I would not have imagined possible.

"I will see you well, little one," Mary would whisper to Thom when she thought Edward and I were distracted. But all of us knew it would be a close thing. If only spring would hurry its arrival!

Toward the end of January Captain Standish's beloved wife Rose breathed her last. While at sea, the two had seldom been far apart. Of late the captain had been preoccupied with mounting a guard and securing the settlement. We had all come to depend most heavily on the stout-hearted soldier, and it grieved me that we were unable to ease the sorrow he felt. I had often witnessed his fierce anger, but it was most startling to see him painfully carrying his good and virtuous wife to the shallop for burial.

"I wonder that any of us survive," Mother told us.

Mistress Standish was the eighth member of our company to die in January, excluding members of *Mayflower's* crew. It seemed a most terrible price to pay for our new homeland.

On shore things had gone little better. Twice the thatch of the common house had caught fire. Both times the anxious men had thought it the work of savages, but more likely sparks from the fireplace had ignited the reeds. The weather was far too hostile for even savages to be about.

The men continued to send fresh meat to *Mayflower*, though, and Thom and Edward improved.

"Food and rest," Mary declared. "That and a breath of spring will cure our ills."

As my brothers were better, I set off to aid Deacon Fuller as he ministered to the ills of the other passengers. Though not a true physician, he knew the healing herbs and mixed them with plentiful prayers.

"These boys will be running through the rigging soon enough," he told Mother as she fretted over a rise in Edward's fever. "Look what color has come back to young Richard's cheeks. He is a wonder, this lad. He is forever about, helping me in my work."

"His father is a devout disciple of a hard day's work," Mother said, smiling for the first time in days as she untangled a knot in a strand of my long blond hair.

"The product does the maker proud," Deacon Fuller said, bowing to her before departing.

February brought no easing of the weather. Cool days and freezing nights sent a fresh wave of despair throughout the women and children aboard ship. Deaths came in pairs more often than not, with illness worst among the servants. Many of them had labored long hours in the open, and with no loved ones to urge them to recovery, most gave themselves up to God's mercy.

I was stronger now, and Master Clarke convinced Father I was capable of handling an oar on one of

Mayflower's boats for a time. I sat nervously beside the oar, for Master Clarke had told me that the man who normally served the post had died but two days before.

Rowing, though hard work, set before me an ocean of fresh air. Sometimes when we had rowed a party ashore, the mate and I would search the shoreline for game. We dreamed of taking a deer, but it was not to be. Master Clarke did shoot some quail in a thicket, and for once we enjoyed a fine dinner.

"Soon we will make our journey home to England," Master Clarke said as we sat alone on the deck toward the end of the month. "You might come along as an apprentice seaman. Or, if you prefer, you could take ship as our cabin boy, serving the officers until such time as you chose to become a mate."

"I must stay to aid Father," I explained.

"But you've no farmer's heart. I can see already the sea's in your blood."

"Honor thy father and thy mother," I said. "It is written in Scripture. My brothers are ill and of small use. Mother has grown weak, and Mary must take over her duties. I am the only one Father can rely on to help him in the fields."

"You are a good and dutiful son, Richard Woodley," Master Clarke said. "*Mayflower* is losing a fine seaman. I hope one day I am blessed of such good fortune as to have such a son."

I was ill accustomed to such praise, and I searched for a reply. "You have shown me great kindness," I told him. "When my heart was full of fear and despair, you spoke of courage and hope. I believe the good fortune will be your son's."

Master Clarke gazed eastward, toward the open sea and the England that lay beyond. I swallowed a sadness growing in my heart, for though *Mayflower* had of late seemed a cold and empty place, I knew I would feel her loss when Master Jones set sail.

I did not know it then, but Mother had asked Master Clarke to occupy me away from the ship. Mary told me much later it was in hope of separating me from the sickness, and perhaps also so that I might not note how pale and sickly Mother herself had become. Finally she took to her bed.

Father visited each day, but there was little he could do. For weeks she had been giving her portions of our meager meals first to me and later to Edward and Thom. Her once lovely teeth had begun to fall out, and her eyes took on a dark and hollow hue. The life was rushing out of her as we all stood helplessly by.

"Lord Jehovah, take me instead," I prayed each night. "She is too much needed."

I searched the marshes for waterfowl while ashore, hoping meat would stave off the fever which had set upon her. But if I found a bird, it was always gone when I returned with someone to shoot it. As for fish, I even tried to capture them with my bare hands.

Father and Master Winslow killed a duck, and Mary stewed it most beautifully. Mistress Winslow had taken ill as well, and we fed both women a goodly portion of broth. But they could not keep the meat on their stomachs.

"You must eat, Mother," I begged. "We cannot go on without you."

"You must always endeavor to do your utmost, Richard," she told me. "For your father, your brothers and sister, for yourself."

"Yes, Mother," I promised.

"As for me, I will not die if God wills it otherwise."

But I had seen too many die. I did not believe God so hardhearted that He would have mothers taken from their children. No, I blamed the cold and the wind and this hostile foreign place that had no softness.

"She grows stronger each day," Father told me as he listened to my verses. "Soon we will all be ashore in our own house, enjoying the bounty of this place."

I did not answer. I had seen no bounty. Only death.

At sea, death comes with the departing tide. So says Master Clarke. I had always imagined that the hour of death would come at dusk. Mother coughed away her life near midday one harsh day in the last week of February.

Elder Brewster spoke words of consolation, and Father read from Scripture and prayed over her body. Mary stayed with Thom and Edward aboard ship while Father and I bore Mother to the small hill where the dead were laid to rest.

We were allowed no markers. Captain Standish thought it unwise to reveal to onlooking savages the calamity which had befallen us. If the Indians had known how weak we were, they could have swept us from the land in a single day.

I wish we had been allowed at least a stone. I had

no place to bring flowers come spring. It was as if Mother had been swallowed by the land.

I wished to cry, but Father insisted on restraint.

"Tears are a weakness, Richard," he said. "She is in God's hands, and no better place can be imagined."

That was fitting, for no better person ever breathed.

That eve I stood beneath a quarter moon on the deck of the ship, searching the dim outline of the distant shore for the hill where my mother lay. Edward was close at my side, still plagued by his cough, but needing as I did to say farewell.

"She will always be with us," I said, using one of Elder Brewster's favorite phrases.

"I should have been the one to die," Edward said.

"She chose to give up her own life that we might have ours," I said sadly. "We must make of ourselves a life worth such sacrifice."

Edward nodded.

"Life is often hard to understand," Mary told me the following morning. "Perhaps if I could read as you do, an answer would come to me."

"I have found none," I said sadly.

She pulled me tightly against her so that the buttons on her bodice stung my face.

"I pray God gives me the strength to see you all grown tall, brother."

I smiled at her, and she hugged me a second time. Father would not have approved such a display, but he was ashore. I slipped my arms around her waist and embraced her.

That night I slept as before with my brothers. I noticed much trembling, and I awoke to find Thom had wrapped one arm around me and the other around Edward. I knew he had been afraid of dying, but now an even greater terror possessed him.

"Mother's gone away," he whispered to me next morn. "Father is often away. You and Mary will never leave, will you?"

I stared at his fearful face and drew him close to me. He was haunted by the notion that we would all go, leaving him alone.

"I might row the longboat to the beach," I told him, "but I will be back by supper. You need not fear, Thom. Father will be aboard for Sabbath, or perhaps we will join him in our house."

"Our house?" Thom asked.

"Yes. Soon we will have a home in Plymouth. We will have pigs to tend. Mary will plant a garden, and we will plant crops."

For a moment his eyes attained a rare luster, but the shine faded, and he stared at the deck. I gripped his tiny hands and hoped he could learn to set aside the awful sadness in his heart. I had abandoned hope of doing so.

"Why did she have to die?" I asked one morning as I stood on Burial Hill. "Why her?"

It was only after voicing my feelings that I realized I was not alone. Kneeling to my left was Captain Standish.

"I have asked myself that question," the captain said. "I thought ye Saints knew every answer."

"Knowledge is not feeling," I said.

"No, it is not," the red-haired captain said, smiling. "Ye'll one day become a most wise man, Richard Woodley."

I noticed that morning even his eyes were red. Tears had been shed. For a moment I wished I had been born among the Strangers. It seemed the life of a Saint was harsh indeed. But upon reflection, I decided we are born to the life God chooses for us. Who are we to question Providence?

Soon it would be spring, and there would be planting. And building. Carving out from this barren place a new life.

I awaited it with hunger.

SIX
SAVAGES

A few days later Father brought us ashore to share the wattle hut he had completed. He said little to us regarding his decision, but I knew he wished to remove us from the scene of Mother's death. Harsh north winds continued to paint the earth with morning frosts, but the embers in our fireplace provided some warmth against the icy nights.

We were allotted such supplies as were our due, and Father was able to shoot birds upon occasion. Mary set about putting the house in order. She also became as a militia captain, commanding Edward, Thom, and me to chop kindling, repair thatch, or complete our lessons.

Since first setting foot on dry land, our company had felt the eyes of savage natives upon us. In late January Master Jones had spotted two Indians spying on *Mayflower* from a small island we had named in honor of our most kind first mate, Master Clarke. A later search of Clarke Island had failed to uncover a single native.

Mid-month we had our first serious encounter. I was gathering water at the spring near our hut when a great shout came from the brook. Men ran in five directions.

"Collect your brothers!" Father shouted to me.

I took my oaken bucket full of water and turned

back toward our home. With my free hand, I motioned to Edward, who was filling the kindling box. Thom was stuffing fern leaves into our beds. The straw used aboard ship had long hence grown brittle and uncomfortable.

"The kindling box is but half full," Mary complained to Edward.

"Father said we should come inside," I told her. "There is much excitement near the brook."

Mary walked with me through the doorway. Captain Standish was assembling the men outside. Father turned toward us.

"It is best you should stay within the house," Father warned. "A party of savages has been seen not far distant."

It was the moment we had all feared. Mary clasped my hand tightly, and Edward leaned against my shoulder.

"Richard, fetch my sword," Father said. "Edward, my powder horn."

We set about locating them amongst Father's possessions near the fireplace. Father took his musket from beside the hearth. I dragged the heavy sword to him, then helped him buckle the great leather belt. Edward placed the powder horn over Father's shoulder. Then Father kissed Mary on her forehead, nodded to us, and set off to join the company.

"We may well be massacred," Mary said, taking a large knife and facing the door. I drew my Spanish dagger from its leather sheath and stood equally ready.

Little Thom looked up at us as if to ask how such a thing could be. Edward coughed nervously. But I

heard Captain Standish's familiar voice bellowing beyond our door.

"Captain Standish has fought Spaniards," I said.
"He will know what course of action to take."

Listening to the captain shout commands lessened
our fears. Soon men set out to explore the neighboring
woodlands. No Indians were located, but Captain
Standish and Francis Cooke, in their haste to return
to our settlement, had left tools in the woods. When
Captain Standish sought to retrieve them, he found
them nowhere in sight.

Instead many strange footprints were discovered
nearby.

"We have long known savages were in the wood,"
Father told us that night as we lay in our beds around
the fire. "This morn while upon a wood-cutting labor,
one of our company spied many men clothed in animal skins walking toward our village. He warned us
to prepare. All was made ready, but the savages chose
not to visit us.

"From this time, we will mount a guard by night.
I bid ye not to venture into the wood without the
company of a man at arms."

We voiced our agreement.

In truth, my dreams were visited that night by terrible creatures, all painted and wearing human bones
about their chests. They spoke strange words, and I
well knew the hunger that filled their eyes. They were
cannibals, eaters of human flesh like those in Master
Clarke's stories.

The next day weapons were cleaned and polished.
The strictist of watches was maintained. All the men

were called together, and with little dissent Captain Standish was formally elected captain of our company.

"What nonsense!" Father declared. "Who else has a soldier's skills or a commander's sense?" Others vowed it important that our company, as free men, should choose who would lead.

Captain Standish only shook his head in dismay and drew the elders aside. As they discussed military affairs, a cry was issued from the guard.

Two savages stood watching all the while. I myself saw them atop a nearby hill. They wore little clothing, and I marvelled that they did not shiver from the cold. Edward thought they were perhaps accustomed to the intemperate climate, but I found it unlikely. We had grown no fonder of the chill air in our months upon the American shores.

Captain Standish and Master Hopkins stepped cautiously forward, setting their arms aside so as to prove peaceful intentions. But in the event, the savages retired into the wood.

We made great entreaties to our Lord that Sabbath, seeking protection from our pagan enemies. The next week Master Jones and Governor Carver began ferrying the great cannon from *Mayflower* to the rise of ground which afterward would be known as Fort Hill.

First the greatest piece, known as a minion, was mounted. Next the two lesser guns were placed. These cannon were long brass barrels fired by touching off charges of powder with a torch. Master Coppin doubted their soundness, for they had not been fired in a great length of time. Even so, all of us felt safer under their protection. It was known the savages often fled at the roar of such great guns.

Hauling the cannons up the hill and placing them correctly required much labor. Afterward a great feasting was made. Master Jones brought a fat goose, and our company collected one plump mallard, a crane, and a dried neat's tongue. Such biscuit as remained was shared, and a plan for fortifying our settlement was discussed.

If it hadn't been for the burials of more of our company, it would have been a good time. February saw seventeen die. The appearance of the savages made us thankful of our precautions in burying by the dead of night. Surely the Indians, seeing our company so greatly reduced, would have attacked.

March brought the first truly fair weather. Mary told me it was not unlike the springtime in Yorkshire she recalled from her childhood. What women remained hoed plots for their gardens and set seeds into the earth. Men prepared the fields for planting.

Even in this time of laboring, we kept our guard vigilant lest we be attacked. Captain Standish drilled the men in musketry and swordplay. It was hoped that when their eyes fell upon our preparations our enemies would shrink from the notion of fighting us.

On a fine Friday in mid-March, the moment we had both waited for and dreaded occurred. Captain Standish was calling the men to the order of arms when a single savage emerged from the wood. This man, tall with long hair as black as night, walked boldly toward us.

Many ran in fear, but I stood in wonder. His dark, proud eyes searched our faces, read our thoughts. He had no beard, and his broad naked chest was as hairless as my own. For clothing he had but a small bit of fringed leather about his waist, suitable for only the barest modesty. His bow, together with two arrows, he set aside.

"Welcome, Englishmen!" he called out to us in an accent that might have belonged to Dorset.

After so many tales of fierce warriors who would eat our flesh, it was difficult to accept this dark-skinned stranger who spoke to us in our native tongue.

He did not tarry in hope of an invitation to come forward. Instead he walked amidst us, waving and smiling as if he were an old acquaintance long estranged.

"Who be ye?" Captain Standish challenged.

"Samoset," the savage answered bravely.

Captain Standish found for Samoset a horseman's cloak to serve as shield against the chill wind. Those in our company who had studied the customs of the Americas called for a meeting. Captain Standish led the Indian to our common house. There Governor Carver treated with Samoset, and much was learned. A piece of mallard was eaten by our visitor, who was a Sagamore or Lord of his tribe. He came from a land far to the north, but he had often journeyed to the cape. He had learned his English from traders and fishermen, and he spoke of many captains who had come before us.

Samoset's gravest disappointment in us was that we possessed no beer. He had acquired a liking for the beverage, and what strong water we had satisfied him but little.

"Aye, his talk rings true enough," Master Clarke told me. "He bears ye no ill."

I was glad to hear it. I was prepared to sleep beside my dagger.

Samoset slept that night in Master Hopkins's hut. Next day we sent him on his way with presents: a knife, a ring, and a bracelet. He appeared most pleased and promised to bring others soon to our village.

Many of our greatest questions were explained by Samoset. The place we had come to was known as Patuxet. The abandoned Indian village had been the home of a tribe by that same name. Four years before a great plague had ravaged the land, likely a pox brought by English seamen. The whole of the Patuxet nation had died.

This tale struck us most profoundly. Even our grief over our many lost companions was almost nothing compared to the death of an entire race.

"Do not sorrow over this grave news, Richard," Elder Brewster bade me. "Do not you see the hand of Providence in this?"

I did not, and I told him.

"These savages were borne away so that we might dwell here. The Lord left their fields that we might plant."

I understood his thoughts, but I prayed God was not so vengeful that he might take my life to prepare a place for some other who might follow.

The day after Samoset's departure being the Sabbath, our company gathered to worship. Our prayers were interrupted by the appearance of a collection of natives near the edge of the wood.

Samoset led the way. With him were five tall Indians, all armed with bows. Captain Standish called for them to halt when still a quarter mile distant. The savages laid down their arms and came forward. Our elders met with them, and the remainder of the company gathered nearby in hope of discovering the purpose of the visit.

I was able to examine them closely. Each wore deerskin about their waists, with long hose like Irish trousers along their legs. The chief among them, a tall, grave-faced man, wore a wildcat's skin on one arm.

Their complexion was dark, not black like the Moorish servants left by former Spanish governors in Leyden, but rather reddish-brown as if they had spent many summers among the Mediterranean islands. One wore feathers in his hair as in a fan. Others wore feathers in back, like foxtails, catching the wind at times. Their beardless faces were painted in blacks and whites and yellows from forehead to chin.

They ate most liberally of the food we offered. Afterward they sang and danced in a manner most wild, screaming so that Thom hid in Mary's skirts and Edward clutched my arm. But I read no anger in their eyes, and it was clear we had nothing to fear from them.

Among their number was one called Massasoit, the leader of all the nearby nations. He brought beaver skins for trade, but because it was the Sabbath, we could not partake in commerce.

Master Carver bade him return to trade another time. Massasoit agreed to do so and further promised he would return the tools taken in the wood.

Samoset passed three days with us, and he might have stayed longer except that the elders did not want the Indians to eat all our stores or learn too much about our defenses. We dispatched Samoset with a hat, a pair of stockings, shoes, a shirt, and a piece of cloth to be put about his waist. Thus we thought we had "civilized" our first savage.

We busied ourselves planting the last of our garden seed the third week of March. On Wednesday, the twenty-first, the last of our company living aboard *Mayflower* came ashore. The ship's carpenter had repaired the shallop, and the crew of the great ship had completed their preparations for the long homeward journey.

The day which followed saw Samoset enter our village again. This time he brought along another Indian. This stranger, who called himself Squanto, proved to be the sole surviving member of the Patuxet people.

At a young age, Squanto had been taken aboard an English ship. Upon reaching a Spanish port, Squanto and others were sold into slavery. Spanish monks rescued him and put him into the service of an Englishman, which is how he learned our language.

To find two natives with so much knowledge and affection for our language and people was most fortunate. These men had come to set into motion much trading. Later Massasoit and his brother, Quadequina, arrived with twenty men. Master Edward Winslow came forward to treat with them.

It was a remarkable sight. Massasoit, whose real name was Ousamaquin, or Yellow Feather, wore his finest garments and brightest feathers. We learned "massasoit" was the word for big chief. His home lay forty miles southwest in a large village called Sowams.

Master Winslow offered many gifts, including a pair of knives and a copper chain with jewels for Massasoit, and a knife and a jeweled earring for Quadequina. Massasoit pleased us much by returning the stolen tools. Afterward the Indians enjoyed some strong water and a quantity of biscuit.

But this was only preparation for greater events. Captain Standish arrived with six musketeers to escort the great chief to the common house. A green rug was set upon the floor, and the men were allowed to sit upon cushions. Governor Carver entered with the beat of a drum and the call of a trumpet.

I was not there, but I learned afterward of the business conducted between our governor and Massasoit. The two leaders kissed hands. Massasoit wore a chain of white bones about his neck which Captain Standish assured us were not human. The chief brought a small bag of tobacco, and a pipe was smoked.

The Indians had painted their faces as before. Massasoit's countenance was a sad red. The others favored yellow and black. After much good talk, spoken through Samoset and Squanto, a great friendship was forged. A treaty was drawn up between us so that it might be known there was to be peace between our peoples.

First it was agreed neither party should bring injury to the other. Any man who did so would be sent to the injured party for such punishment as was deemed merited.

Additionally, any tools stolen were to be returned. Any person making war unjustly upon either of our peoples would be looked upon as an enemy of both. Word would be sent to neighboring tribes so that the alliance would be known, and perhaps an attack prevented. Either group, upon entering the village of the other, would set aside their weapons. A final phrase was added to the effect that by honoring his treaty, Massasoit would be held in high esteem by King James.

It was an agreement well made. Massasoit embraced Master Winslow beside the brook and pledged to return in eight days' time. The Indians would set out corn on the opposite side of the brook and dwell beside us all the summer.

Captain Standish insisted we maintain our guard, but it was little needed. The Indians became great friends to us. They introduced us to the ways of their land, and we learned more things than could be recounted.

"God has indeed blessed us with a great friend," Father told us. "Moses, when cast into the wilderness, was sent no such guide. May we be ever thankful of such a blessing."

I felt much of the same mind. I still remembered the terror that had filled my thoughts, and I wondered if we might have made such a friend as Massasoit had not Samoset spoken our language and dared to venture into our midst.

SEVEN
OUR FRIEND SQUANTO

We greeted the coming of spring with great prayers of thanksgiving. For the first time since arriving in the Americas I felt warm. The air remained crisp and cool at night, but it was nothing to the numbing cold of winter.

Winter had taken half the company. Fifty of our brave companions lay buried on the hill. Few families were spared some loss. Fathers, mothers, daughters, sons—all had gone forth into the hands of God.

The close of March found our company healing. As each day passed, bones grew less brittle. I watched the color return to Edward's cheeks, and Mary was forced to lengthen our sleeves and find new boots for Thom. At times it was possible to hear laughter from the common house.

A great hunger filled me, quite unlike the starvation we had neared in January. Now there was so much work to be done, I never felt satisfied, even though Mary cooked great stews of fowl.

With the food came a restoration of strength. Where once splitting kindling would leave me worn and exhausted, I now could labor all the daylight hours afield. Edward was much the same, for he accompanied me in all my exploits. Thom, being still but six years of age, was kept to the hut, where he helped Mary as he was able.

Our great benefactor during this time was the Patuxet Indian, Squanto. Samoset, our earlier visitor, had returned to his home to the north, but Squanto had adopted our village as his own. Indeed, he had been born on this very ground and knew the wood and fields. He devoted himself to becoming our tutor in all matters of importance.

Our first lesson was in the catching of eels. In the Netherlands, they were most expensive, and I had never tasted one. Eels abounded in the muddy bottom of the brook. We had attempted to catch them earlier, but they did not bite our hooks.

Squanto brought us to the brook each morning. We would remove our boots and stockings and wade into the waters. With our feet we searched the mud for eels. It was strange at first, waiting for the unearthly sensation of the ropelike creatures. Once we located an eel, we would plunge our hands into the shallow stream and capture it. Often we would also fall into the brook, splashing and laughing as the water enveloped us. For a moment we were children, and I thank Squanto as much for the joy we shared as for eels caught.

In such a manner Edward and I caught three eels in a single morn. Mary cooked them in Mother's great iron kettle, adding such seasoning as she had. The meat proved fat and sweet.

Squanto next taught us to hunt birds with stones. We would hide in the marshes and thickets, keeping our movements hidden. When a small duck or partridge appeared, we would lift a heavy stone and throw it at the bird. With good fortune, the stone would break the bird's neck.

When berries appeared on the forest plants, Squanto taught us which ones should be taken. Some could be eaten. Others provided remedies for common ailments. We also dug certain roots near the brook and gathered wild onions and turnips in the wood.

The women recognized familiar simples and herbs among the plants. Mary removed some to her garden and placed them beside the rows planted with seeds Mother had brought from Leyden. Others were ground into powders to be added to our food or kept ready for illnesses.

We made salt from the sea. Great buckets of seawater were collected. As these dried in the sun or were boiled upon a fire, layers of salt collected, which was of much use in the drying of fish.

While we rejoiced of the plentiful food and renewed warmth which visited us, the new season brought another anguish. I was in the wood with Edward when he suddenly became pale as death. I took his hand to lead him homeward, but we had not reached the brook before his breathing became heavy.

"Richard?" he gasped.

I thought for a moment that he would join Mother, but although his breathing was much labored, and he shivered as with a winter chill, I was able to help him to the fields. There Master Winslow took Edward in his arms and carried him to our dwelling.

We were fearful of a new plague, but Mary would hear nonesuch. She located two dried leaves of rosemary and rolled them in her fingers. She next drew the leaves close to Edward's nose. As he inhaled, his breathing eased, and his face grew bright.

"Our new physician," Father proclaimed.

"I haven't read books," Mary boasted, "but neither am I ignorant. Mistress White is teaching me the herbs."

Though Father chastised such prideful utterings, I could tell he was proud of her. Henceforth Edward carried a leaf of rosemary with him when we took to the wood. When he grew faint, he would breathe its aroma and renew himself.

As the trees regained their leaves, we began our preparations for the planting. Already the fields had been made ready for what wheat and barley we had seed to plant. A few acres of peas were to be set out. From Squanto we learned it was yet early to plant the corn.

In late March Master Carver was reelected our governor. Much work was carried out in the village, and Father planned a cottage to replace the small hut we now inhabited. Great barrels were brought ashore from *Mayflower* to be filled with fresh water for the ship's voyage back to England.

I found my heart growing heavy as the final preparations were made for *Mayflower's* departure. I had come to look upon the ship as both friend and protector, as our home for so long a time. On the eve of her sailing, I found myself walking with Master Clarke on the beach.

"You will be asea once again on the morrow," I said, staring out past the horizon, imagining it was possible to see the distant coast of England.

"Aye, by sundown we will be out to sea," he said.

"It is a long way to Southampton."

" 'Tis but another ocean to cross. To a sailor, it is as green a pasture as yon field."

"You can't plant seed in an ocean," I told him.

"Aye, but a sailor's no planter. He is a reaper at times, for he harvests fish from the sea. Nay, more often he's a wanderer with no home port, cast upon a wind."

"I fear it would be a life I would grow weary of."

"There is a weariness, Richard Woodley, but there is a joy of discoveries, fair harbors, and new lands."

"Like this one?"

"Aye."

"Have you never found a place you wished to make your home?"

"I have a home: the sea."

"And a family?"

"Aye, my mates. Upon occasion I acquire others."

"Boys who listen to tales?"

"Aye, and those who steer a ship or caulk a boat."

I found myself smiling, and I wish my tongue had been able to give him my thanks.

"Ye would have made a fine sailor," he told me. "But I see the heart of a farmer. Ye wish to grow things."

"Perhaps I shall grow myself," I said, hoping to lighten the mood.

"I never knew a boy to stand so tall," Master Clarke said. "If the winds were to blow me to the Americas years hence, I would find you a great man, Lord of the Manor or the like."

"There's greater likelihood I'll be a poor farmer, but you will be welcome to share my table."

"Men who weather the storm are bound by it," he said, setting his great rough hand upon my head. "We should drink a pint of ale in parting, but alas, there is none to be had. I bid ye a fair harvest and a better winter."

"May you find the winds fair to England," I replied. Reluctantly I watched him walk to the ship's boat.

The next morn, the fifth day of April, *Mayflower* hoisted sail and set out on her return voyage. Master Jones, who had been our stalwart supporter, bade us farewell with a cannon salute. I thought I spied Master Clarke in the rigging, watching those of us who stood on the beach. But one seaman is like another from a great distance.

I had little time in the days to come to concern myself with Master Clarke or *Mayflower*. His many kindnesses would abide with me always, but just as I had set behind me those friends left in Leyden, I now put aside those aboard *Mayflower* or laid to rest on Burial Hill.

Squanto had us occupied at the brook, constructing a wall of thatch across the mouth of the stream. The water continued its flow, but our weir was such that any fish seeking the sea would be held as in a net.

When all was complete, a great multitude of alewives, fish something like herrings, were trapped. We collected these fish in baskets. Some we cooked to ease our hunger. The greater part Squanto bade us keep for the planting.

We did not understand in the beginning. But Squanto did not keep us in ignorance for long. All old enough to walk were called to the fields next morn. Squanto took a pole of sorts and made a hole in the earth. Then he let bits of his corn fall into this hole. He next made a small hill of the earth and placed three alewives in a pattern that put me in mind of a Y.

"To make the corn grow tall," Squanto explained as he laid the fish on the earth. "Field feeds the corn. Fish feed the field."

I thought it must be some pagan religious practice, but Master Carver said it was not unlike the manure spread upon the fields by farmers in England. It would make our soil rich and the corn bountiful.

Day after day we planted the seed corn Captain Standish and his fellows had dug from the strange mound on Cape Cod. Squanto told us Indians buried the seed corn so that it could not be eaten in the depth of winter. In satisfying its hunger, the tribe might find itself without seed come spring and be doomed to starvation the following winter.

Our nightly guard faced little challenge from Massasoit's band, who had taken up residence on the far side of the brook. A greater problem was the many rotting fish in the cornfields. First birds and later wolves came to partake of the fish. Many a crow was shot, and several times we encountered wolves near enough our homes to merit concern.

It was also in April that a great loss was attended our company. Our able governor, Master John Carver, took ill in the fields.

He raised his hand to his head as if there were a great pain there. Then he fell. We rushed to his aid and bore him to his house. Though Elder Brewster and others prayed most heartily at his sickbed, the governor never spoke again. His eyes seemed bright and thoughtful until the end a few days later. We buried him as an honored member of our community. Captain Standish led the militia in a full salute.

There was much discussion about who should succeed Master Carver as governor. Some thought Elder Brewster would be a wise choice, but others thought it an occupation for a younger man. Master William Bradford, having no family at present and being highly educated, was selected. Master William Allerton was chosen to assist him.

It was a provident choice. Master Bradford took able charge of our affairs, and his abilities proved of great merit. Master Allerton, having been a merchant, was useful in organizing the community. A tailor, he had generously given many of us shoes and clothing. So it was that when a thing was asked of us in turn, no one complained.

In mid-May the first marriage was celebrated in our new home. Master Edward Winslow, whose beloved Elizabeth had passed on shortly after my mother, took as his second wife Mistress Susanna White, widowed in February. Master Winslow took into his heart and home Mistress White's two sons, the youngest of whom had been born upon our arrival in the Americas.

Afterward many men who had lost their wives to the illness wedded the widows of their fellows. In this manner children came to be provided with both mother and father once more.

I believe Father would have taken a new wife were it not for Mary. She was as an angel, tending our needs and tempering our spirits. Her one great complaint was in the size and nature of our hut, and so it was that Father chose to construct a cottage.

Had there been fewer than the five of us, I doubt such an endeavor would have been attempted. Father determined Edward and Thom could tend the fields with the others, leaving me to aid him in cutting trees for stout walls. Mary was kept occupied by her garden and other duties that would have broken the back of any less able person.

Long did we labor in the wood, cutting great trees and trimming their branches. Having no draft animals, we were forced to pull the logs the great distance homeward on our own shoulders.

Father enlisted the aid of others in the framing of the cottage. The great logs were first sawed into beams. These were squared and rived as was the custom in England. A large fireplace of stone and clay was constructed. We then turned to sawing planks for the walls.

It was to be a grand place. Save for the tall house built by Master Winslow and the cottage constructed by Elder Brewster, our dwelling was the equal of any. Father's house had a wide hall, with a smaller room off to one side. A loft was constructed overhead for the storage of tools and goods. The loft was also to provide sleeping quarters for Edward, young Thom, and myself.

During this labor I became most talented with a saw and maul. Father and I needed aid in joining the corner walls, but for using wedge and maul, no better were to be found upon the plantation.

We devoted ourselves to the cottage whenever we were not needed in the fields. Father had also his militia drills to attend. But as the July heat descended upon us, all four walls stood in place. We had only to thatch the roof for our new home to be complete.

The cottages that were replacing the meager huts of Plymouth were not the only signs of change to be found. A palisade was completed enclosing our dwellings. Atop the hill where our cannons rested, a meeting house was built. A wall was constructed above to serve as a small fort in time of peril.

Perhaps the greatest change was Squanto. He had first come to us as a half-naked savage. For his many kindnesses he had been given a fine suit of clothes, complete with a horseman's cloak with red lace about the edges. He took on the stature of a duke, bowing to those of us he had chased through the brook but a month afore.

In July Squanto led Master Winslow and Master Hopkins southward in search of the large village where Massasoit made his capital. They were gone more than a week, and we feared for their safety. Upon returning, Master Winslow told of the terrifying plague that had brought death to the Patuxet people and left other villages a graveyard of unburied skulls and bones.

Masters Winslow and Collins met with great success in their commerce with Massasoit. There was promise of much beaver trade, and although the Indian dwellings had filled both Master Winslow and Master Hopkins with a great desire to return to Plymouth, much progress was made in relations between our peoples. A warrior from Massasoit's council, a tall Indian named Hobomok, was sent to live with us. Hobomok would speak for Massasoit in all affairs and would seek him out should we be endangered.

We sought Massasoit's aid in making peace with any tribe that might threaten us. Master Winslow had offered to pay the Cape savages for the corn we had taken, and Massasoit promised to bring the matter before the chiefs of those tribes, known as the Nauset people.

In the event, we were to hear from the Nauset all too soon. That same month young John Billington, aged seven years, disappeared from the wood. No great alarm came of this in the beginning. John's brother Francis had journeyed some miles into the forest not long before, discovering a large lake to the west.

The Billingtons were less than pious people, given to taking the Lord's name in vain and failing to keep the Sabbath. Aboard ship they almost exploded a powder keg that would have sent us all to the bottom of the Atlantic. But when days passed without John's return, we feared perhaps some savages might have enjoyed a feast upon him.

Word was sent to the Indians. We wished the boy's return. A reply came. John had made his way twenty miles south to an Indian plantation known as Manomet. From there he had been taken to the Nauset.

Governor Bradford sent the shallop to bring John back. An offer to make payment for the corn we had taken was sent, along with such goods as were thought proper in recompense for the kindness the Nauset people had done in tending John. A great peace was made with the Nauset as a result.

These Nauset people had suffered most cruelly at the hands of English sailors. Some seven years before, a certain Captain Thomas Hunt had seized thirty savages while on a fishing voyage. Seven of the Indians were members of the Nauset tribe. The captives were taken to Spain and sold as slaves in the same manner as had befallen Squanto.

Our people were glad of the safe return of John Billington. Later a body of Indians arrived from Cape Cod to receive our payment for the corn. Much feasting and celebrating followed. So it was that our neighbors were satisfied as to our intentions.

Midsummer found us strong and prosperous, with the corn plants reaching skyward and promising ample harvest. Sabbath meetings turned to the Psalms and away from Job and Lamentations. It was a fine time, blessed by golden sunlight and good health.

Our cottage complete, Father turned his hand to making benches and stools for the hall. He shot much fowl with his musket, and we dried fish against our winter needs.

"Bless this food to our nourishment, this day to our labors, and this company to Thy purposes," Father prayed each morn. It appeared to me his prayer was answered.

EIGHT
THROUGH GOD'S GRACE,
A HOME

No better season had I known than that first summer
in our new home. The bright sunlit days raised our
spirits and cast aside the chills and despairs that had
lingered from a most desperate winter. Food had never
been so plentiful, and as we explored the nearby waters,
we learned to harvest the sea as we did the land. New
creatures as big as kettles, with great red claws larger
than my hand, were captured in the ocean shallows.
We also came to know the best season for digging
mussels.

Much of July and August I passed in the fields with
my brothers. Father would often be there as well, but
he had his duties with the militia, his carpentry and
hunting to attend. At first we busied ourselves thin-
ning the stalks. Squanto told us the plants each required their own space, and so we plucked from the
ground with our hands such plants as crowded others.
Later our task was to remove the wild plants that in-
truded on our fields.

Our company was blessed with many farmers, and
these men became our teachers. From them we learned
to distinguish between the leaves of the young pea
and barley plants and those native grasses which would
rapidly have overgrown our fields. We also learned

the short quick strokes with which a hoe could take such grasses from the earth.

It was a great trial to watch the wheat, barley, and young pea plants, for they did poorly. I especially missed the bright flowers of the peas, the sweet smell of their blossoms. The stalks of the Indian corn, though, were a wonder. By the close of July the plants stood above my shoulders.

A great game for Edward and Thom was to hide themselves among the stalks, knowing as they did their yellow hair would blend with the corn plants. They had great sport of me, flinging small pebbles upon my head when I was about the hoeing. I would on occasion catch sight of a bit of jerkin or the dark leather of a shoe. At such times a most grievous revenge would be administered.

Father had no great patience with our play.

"A man must be about his business," he would tell us. "Do not give yourselves to the devil's bidding."

But in truth I believe it did his heart no little good to hear our laughter. In the time following Mother's dying there had been too heavy a sadness upon our house. Always the remembrance of her loss was with us. Now at last we felt we might be assured that no other among us would be taken. In Sabbath prayers the times of hardship were always remembered, that our present good fortunes might be better celebrated.

When we were most solemn, Squanto would appear with sundry new adventures to raise our spirits. He introduced us to Patuxet games, stalking contests where one might follow another in silence through the wood. Captain Standish chose to train us in the use of the

English quarterstaff. Also lessons in the handling of the shallop's sail or the rowing of her oars would occupy our days. And when the sun set, Father would have us study our verses.

My favorite among the lessons was that of fishing. Although we still had no small hooks, Squanto taught us to make from the limb of a tree a short and narrow staff perhaps four hands in length. The end was sharpened like the point of a spear. We would then take to the brook, plunge our heads beneath the water, and drive our staff through the sides of any fish we could see.

It was far from simple, as holding one's breath is a true art. The brook's bottom was a collection of rocks and water plants, and fish would often be hidden from view. Once I stabbed at movement and nearly caught Edward's foot. But in time we learned the game well. It would bring great rewards with the return of winter.

Our greatest challenge that summer was the thatching of our new house. Grass and reed were gathered, and ropes were stretched across the roof beams. Mary and Thom bound the reed in bundles, and Edward and I climbed to the top of the wall and labored at the difficult task of weaving the thatch.

Father told us a house in England would be thatched each half score of years. As we bent ourselves to the task, I prayed we would not suffer the calamity of fire which would make a second thatching necessary in the near future.

We stood atop the house for entire days, bare to the waist so that the heat might not overcome us. Edward's face would swell, and his breathing would grow labored, but the rosemary leaves revived him. As for our color, great patches of scarlet rose upon our faces, shoulders, and arms so that we slept most miserably.

"Sunburn," Squanto told us. He disappeared into the wood and returned with hard red berries. These he ground to a powder which he mixed with fish oil to make a most noxious liquid. Mary rubbed it onto our bodies, and the fire was extinguished. After a time the red turned to brown, and we suffered no more.

We devoted many days to our new roof. A fine thatch was woven which would keep off the rain and shield us from the worst of the winter winds.

In August Father decided that I should learn the use of a musket. Nearing my fourteenth year, I was yet so slight of frame that my carrying a sword was nearly impossible. I could rest a musket upon an iron pin, however.

I studied with Captain Standish and Master Hopkins, whose son Giles was but a year my senior. Although he was one of the Strangers, Master Hopkins had learned much about the New World. He had joined the first explorations, and now he had come to be among the most reliable men in the company.

Giles was taller and much stronger than I, but he was no abler a student. He often spilled his powder in a most dangerous manner while I carefully filled the flashpan with the proper number of grains. I was a most skillful loader. Only in aim did I fall short. My arms could not steady the great iron barrel of the musket, and I was as apt to shoot clouds as the target.

"Arms have a habit of growing, lad," Captain Standish said as I continued to miss my mark. "Ye've a keen enough eye. What say ye to a hunt?"

I little expected such an opportunity and was at once filled with excitement.

"Have ye seen deer in yon wood?" he asked.

"Many a time," I told him. "Squanto has taught us to stalk them, but I do not know if they would stand still for such a long time as it takes our match to burn the powder."

"We have time to discover that," Master Hopkins said. "I have a fondness for meat."

In the event, Master Hopkins and Giles were preoccupied with other affairs, and it was Father who took to the wood with Captain Standish and myself. I was not allowed a musket, which was considered too much a burden for one not yet fourteen. Instead I was sent through the thickets to scout a suitable target for the men's musketry.

I had little faith that we would find deer. It was approaching midday, and always before I had seen deer beside the brook in the morning or toward nightfall. I held hope of catching sight of wild turkey, for Love Brewster and young Joseph Mullins had spoken of the exalted taste of the great birds.

I stepped lively and carefully through the thick nests of vines and ferns. Briars tore at my stockings, and I knew I would receive harsh reprimand at Mary's hand for the mending that would be needed to restore them. But though my ears caught many sounds, they located no game save a tortoise, and I thought it unlikely quarry for musketeers.

Twice I rejoined Father and the captain.

"I am proven a most unworthy hunter," I told them.

But they urged me to try once more.

I had nearly lost hope when at last I saw a dark shadow in the forest ahead. Bending low so that I merged with the wood, I waited for the creature to come near. Finally, from the edge of a small meadow, three small deer came into view.

I could scarcely still my heart as I retired through the vines to where Father and Captain Standish awaited. When I found them, my voice failed me and I could only gesture to follow.

"What manner of game have you spotted?" Father asked.

I made an outline of antlers, and Captain Standish held my shoulder so that I became still. I caught my breath and told them of the three animals.

"Make no such haste as to spoil the shot," the captain said. "Move slowly and to purpose."

I nodded my head, then led the way through the trees.

The deer were still in clear view when we reached the meadow, but there remained much to be done. Father and the captain sank their iron supports into the ground, then powdered and primed their weapons. When all was made ready, they struck their matches and waited for the muskets to roar.

Father's piece discharged first. Its ball shattered a limb above the head of the first deer. Captain Standish's shot struck low. The deer took flight, and we were left with not so much as a shadow for our efforts.

But the captain's sharp eyes detected a rabbit, and moments later he had shot the small creature.

For our own part, Father was able to shoot a fat mallard at the brook so that we had roast duck for dinner.

"A matchlock musket is no equal to a running deer," Father said as we plucked the bird. "Yet it makes short work of waterfowl."

My musketry was little threat to either. But Captain Standish praised my efforts and offered me a post with the militia.

"Surely not as a swordsman," Father said.

"Nay, but each army must have its drummer, and yon drummer Henry Kane can raise a musket with the best of us," the captain said. "Here, lad, put thy hand to these."

Captain Standish handed me two long drumsticks, but no drum.

"And the drum?" I asked.

"When ye can carry the tune on a solid log, we'll offer ye our drum."

I was most delighted with my new duty, but I fear the remainder of our company looked upon me as a cross to bear. I beat my sticks against anything that moved, not excluding certain of my friends and brothers. For a time I had the use of Mother's great kettle but it was thought my fearful sounds were frightening the birds from the shore. Afterward I was left with one of Father's stools and a flat crate that had brought part of Master Winslow's printing tools from the Netherlands.

"Must we truly have a drummer if so great a price must be paid?" Mistress Hopkins inquired.

"A cow bell is more melodious," Mary declared.

But in time I gained mastery over the sticks, and Captain Standish turned over to my care the large snare drum brought from England. Henceforth, I was summoned whenever the militia was to be called to arms or beckoned to drill. I also would spread the alarm should fire break out or ship be sighted. It was a great responsibility, and I came to be highly regarded and not a little envied by the other boys.

August passed in long days of fishing and tending the fields, beating the drum at musketry drills, and helping Father lay boards for the floor of what would be the loft in our cottage. September dawned rich and golden. The cornfields were full of giant stalks with husks as long as my forearm. Squanto showed us how to determine the ripeness. When it was finally the moment for harvest, we all gathered in the fields to collect our crop.

With only fifty surviving members of our company, and many of those mere infants, the burden each of us bore was great. Some of the men mounted the guard, and others were engaged in trading for beaver with the Indians. I myself labored from the sun's first dawning to near dark.

"I do not see why the traders should escape toiling in the fields," I complained bitterly to Father.

"Our crops might sustain us, Richard," Father told me with rare patience, "but without goods to barter to England, our benefactors certainly would send none of the goods we so desperately need. Beaver hats bring a high price in London, and without a fishing trade, we have great need of the enterprise."

"I would gladly set off for Massasoit's village," I told him.

"Yes," Father said, grinning at the spirit of adventure blazing in my eyes. "But you have such talent in the fields that it would be sinful to waste it."

I spoke no more of it thereafter, for I could tell he was searching his memory for an appropriate verse to add to my lessons.

While we harvested the corn, Mary brought our midday meal to us in the fields. Father would give leave for Thom to sleep a bit afterward, for he was sorely tired from the work. Edward and I grew weary as well, but not wishing to be thought sloth, we would continue so long as Father instructed.

While we labored in the cornfields, others carried scythes to cut the barley. Though the corn had grown in great bounty, the barley was a disappointment. Many among our company had a great hunger for that familiar grain, and they had thought to brew beer. Now there was little hope of either, for the barley crop was stunted and scant, though we had devoted a fourth of our acreage to it.

The peas were so poor as to not merit gathering. They had come up parched at the blossom, and it was thought they had been put to ground too late. Some said the seeds had taken in salt water. It was worth little discourse.

God greatly blessed us with the corn harvest. No man can doubt our Lord set great burdens in our path.

Speedwell was a grave peril, and our arrival late in the year brought death and sickness. But in our time of need, He provided us with seed for corn and with Squanto and Samoset, who taught us how to sow and when to reap. Had we not the seed, we could well have faced a second winter of starvation, with no ship as refuge and no hope of a better future.

While Edward and I tore the husks from the tall cornstalks, others built great racks for drying. Squanto explained some of the fresh corn could be eaten, but the remainder should be stored for winter needs. Still another portion should be buried as seed for next year.

In the early days of harvest, I cut husks from the stalks. Later, after the smaller stalks had been emptied, the men tended that work and left us with the duty of carrying the husks back to the drying racks.

Twenty acres had been seeded with corn, and I dare not number the stalks which grew upon those acres. One, two, sometimes three husks grew on each stalk. It appeared to me more than once that we harvested enough corn to fill the *Mayflower* twice over. But perhaps it only seemed so.

Day after day we toiled at bringing the corn to the racks. Later, when dried, it was taken to the storehouse.

"A man should labor with a joyous heart," Father told us.

"My heart is light, Father," I told him. "It is my feet that are heavy."

"You would prefer to be back in Leyden, leading your cart through the streets?" he asked.

I remembered the dogs tearing at my legs and

frowned. No, this might bring a weariness, but it would pass. In this new land there was the promise of better years to come.

Edward and I, being about the same height, placed a pole upon our shoulders, which bore a basket of husks. Others paired off in like manner. We transported much corn this way, but it was no simple task. I, walking in back, rarely saw the ground and thus stumbled over rocks or small animal holes. Once I rolled over a small hill and found myself buried in corn husks.

When we finished such days, I sank into the comfort of my bed in the loft. My shoulders would ache as if they bore, as those of Atlas had, the weight of the heavens. Such comparison with a pagan god would have angered Father, but I learned of it from Elder Brewster. In my great weariness, I often grew less careful in my thinking.

I do not know how many days we spent gathering in our harvest. There was a satisfaction to the work, though. Squanto showed us how to roast the fresh corn upon coals in the earth, and we found it tasted wonderful. It did not seem fit to spoil such a rare delight with boiled fish, so Father and I set off one morn to shoot a mallard for our table.

I still lacked the strength of Captain Standish, though I fast approached his stature. But Father helped me set the gun upon its rod and await the arrival of such fowl as might frequent the brook in the hour before the sun broke the horizon.

We stood beside the musket for what seemed to me a lifetime, careful to keep the powder dry in its pan and the match ever ready. Finally a great white goose appeared close by. Father struck the match, and I guided the barrel of the musket toward the bird. A great roar followed. The air filled with smoke, and my eyes stung most horribly. A terrible squawking spread along the pond.

When the smoke settled, I found to my amazement a pair of geese had been shot. Dozens more still occupied the brook's far bank. Father reloaded the musket while I retrieved the birds. Soon we were firing again. We returned home with our game bag filled with four geese—enough food for a week or more.

As I plucked feathers, carefully saving them to fill a bed, Father cleaned his musket. It was still early, and the sun had scarcely chased the night from view. It had been a great while since we had shared a moment alone.

"You've grown tall," Father said, resting his hand on my shoulder as I plucked feathers.

"Not so tall as Mary."

"There is time."

"Father, were you tall as a boy?"

"Nay, not so tall as I would have chosen to be. Woodley men have never been so tall as some."

"What have Woodley men been?"

"Farmers for as far back as I know. My grandfather built the house where I was born. He had been a bowman in the king's service and was granted land in recompense. Woodleys have been pious. We read the Scripture and keep the Sabbath."

"I study my verses."

"And read well for a boy with little schooling. There's a musical side to you as well. Your mother would have liked that. She was much of a mind to play the harpsichord as a girl. She sang like a lark."

I remembered her voice and shuddered. Father noticed and gripped my shoulder tightly.

"I wish your mother could have seen you this morn," Father said softly. "She would have been most proud. Often I thought she favored Edward, his being sickly as an infant, but it was always you, Richard, she thought had the makings of an elder. 'See Richard keeps at his Latin,' she would urge me. I wish I was a better educated man myself that I might give you more. But perhaps Elder Brewster can give you what Latin you need."

"A man won't need Latin in this land," I told Father.

"Educated men know Latin."

"Squanto is educated, and he has not been to schools," I said. "I will learn all about this country. I might learn the Indian languages."

"We would no longer need Squanto."

"I would not be so good a student as that," I said, looking away a moment as my face turned red. "We will soon be exploring other places, and there should be one among us who can treat with the Indians."

"The elders have spoken these very words," Father told me. "I will have discourse with Elder Brewster. I pray you tend such study better than you learn your Scripture."

I thought I witnessed a smile on his stern face. And as he spoke more about our future, I felt very close to him. It had not always been so, but perhaps it was not his doing that had made it that way.

As we set out into the fields after breaking our fast, I walked with a lively step. Our harvest was nearly in and our cottage built. Not even the first chill northern winds could dampen my spirit.

NINE
THE LORD'S BOUNTY

With the harvest gathered, our attention turned to preparing ourselves for the winter. Waterfowl descended upon the brook in the hundreds, and most of the daylight hours we hunted. The fishing was good as well. What was not eaten could be salted and dried for later use.

In the eve, we gathered beside the fire. I studied my verses or aided Edward with his reading. Often we would draw letters on Thom's slate so that he would come to recognize a *C* as a *C* and not a *P* or a *K*. Father would sit opposite us, working the surface of what was to be the side of a chest. When the moment arrived for the joining, I applied the drift until Father was able to insert the pegs which would hold the chest together. The hinges I would do myself, for Father had no eye with a square, and the work would have to be redone.

"He has the makings of a carpenter," Father told Captain Standish as I called the company to drill.

"Aye, but I fear the heart of a cavalier," the captain said, laughing as I beat the drum.

That autumn we devoted ourselves much to the order of arms. Captain Standish was a harsh taskmaster, and his face would often redden when some member of the company scattered his powder or dropped his shot. Of many things we were lacking, but of powder there was plenty. We practiced upon our musketry most diligently. Even the captain agreed our marksmanship was the equal of any company of English musketeers.

In late September it was decided that ten men would set out in the shallop to trade for beaver. We hoped that a good cargo of fur shipped to England would encourage merchants to sponsor additional colonists. Our numbers wanted increasing, and some amongst us had left behind wives and children.

Squanto guided the party, and they returned with many wondrous coats of beaver and sundry other furs. It was a fortune in commerce attained at the cost of some metal pots and various tools. Afterward Indians from many tribes came to barter furs for such goods as we had to trade, and great friendships were established between our peoples.

Whenever savages were about, Captain Standish had us stand to arms. The roar of our musketry and the beating of the drum greatly impressed the savages. The captain would make targets from corn stalks shaped in the manner of men. As the shapes were torn by our shot, the savages trembled. I sensed there was less likelihood of attack thereafter.

October brought a chill across New Plymouth. The first touch of winter was carried on the wind, and the trees exchanged their cloaks of Lincoln green for bright orange and scarlet. Seven houses now stood along the narrow lane that split the two halves of the town. Four, including the storehouse and the meeting house, had been built for common usage. Our own cottage and two others were complete. Such other families and single men as had not finished cottages would weather the harsh winter months in their huts.

I was glad of our cottage. Though the loft was cold enough in spite of the great hearth, Edward and I had filled our beds with goose down and small bits of cloth so that comfort could be found there. And little wind found its way through the thick thatch.

There was a sense of home as well. Of our father's children, only Mary remembered another place as home. We had dwelt in many rooms in Leyden, always atop a shop or behind a wealthy merchant's house. This cottage was our own. Our hands had put its planks in place. Our labors had built the furniture, the roof. The herbs and berries about the hall had been gathered by us, and the dried fish and fowl were taken by us from the brook and field.

We were visited in October by a great congregation of Indians. Amidst them stood Massasoit, the sachem or great chief who had first granted us a treaty. Governor Bradford was both pleased and alarmed at Massasoit's arrival, being most glad of his continued friendship but knowing also the strain on our supplies that so many unexpected guests would entail.

"It is fitting we should gather together with our friends to celebrate God's most bountiful blessings," Elder Brewster proclaimed. "Let us have feasting and good company."

Massasoit was pleased when Squanto explained the words. But the chief did not wish to impose upon our hospitality. He sent men into the wood to hunt, as we did ourselves. The Indians returned with five deer, while we brought a great quantity of ducks and geese, several plump wild turkeys and a goodly quantity of eels. The children gathered shellfish at the beach, and the women cooked herbs and baked bread.

When the day arrived for our feast, we all assembled together, red man and white, so that the food might be blessed to our nourishment and good health.

"And let it be remembered hereafter the friendship of our people," Governor Bradford spoke, "that those who follow might live in peace and prosperity."

Squanto translated the words, and the Indians responded with a great cry of approval.

I never in my history knew a time when so much food was assembled in one place. Platters of roasted duck and steaming kettles of clams stood beside huge turkeys and great steaks of venison. Succulent eels and brook trout were nearby. Corn aplenty and loaves of bread were passed among us. Leeks and watercress, sallet herbs, wild plums, and dried berries were present. A strong, sweet wine of native grapes had been prepared for drink. Such feasting was most impressive for a people who so short a time ago had been starved. Indeed, the Lord's hand was seen in this good fortune.

It was a time of great sharing. Massasoit's people and our own exchanged goods. Some of his warriors showed the use of the bow while Captain Standish demonstrated the order of arms. The children engaged each other in contests of skill and strength. The Indian boys appeared taller and stronger, and they played in a most uncivilized manner. I fear they offered us but few chances of success.

As the celebrating spread throughout our company,

I watched many faces long darkened by toil and hardship, pain and loss. A smile appeared here. A bit of laughter was heard there. Planting had been a time of beginning, of growing. But it seemed to me that perhaps harvest was a different manner of beginning for us. For on this day I saw people begin to hope again.

I left Edward wrestling with an Indian boy and walked for a time alone. At first I was unsure as to what my destination might be, but my feet never lacked purpose. They bore me finally to Burial Hill. There, amidst the unmarked ground, we had laid my mother. When I arrived, I found I was not alone. Others, some alone, some with children, walked slowly, silently nearby.

Father was there. His face was solemn, and he smiled only when he noted my presence.

"She would be proud of us, I think," Father said softly as he took my hand and led the way toward the beach.

Yes, I thought. She would be.

I remembered how great a body we had been coming across the Atlantic. The long voyage streamed through my memory. I saw again the laughter, then the tears, the adventure, and the sadness.

Glancing back at Burial Hill, I thought of the great sacrifices that had been made. But here we stood, in a land we would call our own, strong and confident. With God's continued grace we would build a truly new world, different than all that had gone before.

"Once I wondered why I came here," Father said. "I brought your mother to her death, and you children were not so far removed from the grave yourselves."

"Why did we come, Father?" I asked.

"So that your children, and their children, would find a better life," he told me. "And for that we have endured great hardship and suffered terrible loss."

He turned back toward the hill, and I gripped his hand tightly. Yes, those who lay on that hill had paid a great price. But their sacrifice had allowed us to survive. And now, we would build a new, brighter future in this new land of ours.

ACKNOWLEDGMENTS

No writer of historical fiction can practice the craft without borrowing from the wonderful work of talented historians. I owe a special debt to the dozens of research librarians who have put up with my requests for this text or that from farflung Garland, Texas, and to the talented writers of those books and articles.

No writer on life in early Plymouth should fail to take advantage of the re-created village at Plimoth Plantation—a living history farm and settlement open to the public outside modern Plymouth, Massachusetts. The museum there has well-researched displays, and I found the staff eager to answer questions about even the most obscure facet of life in early Plymouth.

Plimoth Plantation's greatest charm is that it offers the visitor a chance to briefly explore life as it was in the 1620s village. In three trips, I spoke with Edward Winslows and young John Billingtons aplenty, attended musket drill, had a tour of an herb garden, and even tasted some fish stew. I am deeply grateful for the dedicated people who gave up their summers to help me gain insights into our common past. This book would not be the same without their generous gifts of time and interest.

Bobbing about nearby at a pier in Plymouth proper is *Mayflower II*—a replica of the original sailing ship which repeated the perilous crossing of the Atlantic in 1957. Thanks to the exhibits on the pier, the knowledgeable staff aboard, and the ship's re-creators, I was able to glimpse firsthand the confining nature of that Atlantic crossing.

I am equally appreciative to the people of both Plymouths—American and English—for the care they have taken in preserving and honoring the past. On the train out from London, I was treated to a delightful travelogue, especially through Somerset and Devon, conducted with typical English thoroughness by a total stranger. I was likewise entertained on the west shore of the Atlantic by Plymouth residents who told me stories of Burial Hill ghosts and showed me relics left by grandmothers' grandmothers.

Knowledge does not always come from the pages of books, but I include in the bibliography those volumes which were of special help to me during my research. Thanks to the authors.

SELECTED BIBLIOGRAPHY

Baker, William A. *The New Mayflower: Her Design and Construction.* Barre, Massachusetts: Barre Publishing Co., 1958.

Bradford, William. *Of Plymouth Plantation, 1620–1647.* Introduction by Francis Murphy. New York: The Modern Library, 1981.

Brown, Elizabeth Myers, ed. *The Pilgrims and Their Times.* Columbus, Ohio: Highlights for Children, 1974.

Loeb, Robert H., Jr. *Meet the Pilgrims.* Garden City, N.Y.: Doubleday & Co., 1979.

Marshall, Cyril Leek. *The Mayflower Destiny.* Harrisburg, Pa.: Stackpole Books, 1975.

Moore, George N. and G. Willard Woodruff, eds. *The Pilgrims' Journal.* North Billerica, Mass.: Curriculum Associates, 1975.

Morrison, Samuel Eliot. *The European Discovery of America: The Northern Voyages—A.D. 500–1600.* New York: Oxford University Press, 1974.

—————.*The Story of the "Old Colony" of New Plymouth, 1620–1692.* New York: Alfred A. Knopf, 1956.

Rutman, Darrett B. *Husbandmen of Plymouth.* Boston: Beacon Press, 1967.

Willison, George F. *The Pilgrim Reader.* Garden City, N.Y.: Doubleday & Co., 1953.